SHIRLEY JACKSON

We Have Always Lived in the Castle

With an Afterword by Joyce Carol Oates

PENGUIN BOOKS

PENGUIN CLASSICS

Published by the Penguin Group
Penguin Books Ltd, 80 Strand, London WC2R 0RL, England
Penguin Group (USA) Inc., 375 Hudson Street, New York, New York 10014, USA
Penguin Group (Canada), 90 Eglinton Avenue East, Suite 700, Toronto, Ontario, Canada M4P 2Y3
(a division of Pearson Penguin Canada Inc.)
Penguin Ireland, 25 St Stephen's Green, Dublin 2, Ireland (a division of Penguin Books Ltd)
Penguin Group (Australia), 707 Collins Street, Melbourne, Victoria 3008, Australia
(a division of Pearson Australia Group Pty Ltd)
Penguin Books India Pvt Ltd, 11 Community Centre, Panchsheel Park, New Delhi – 110 017, India
Penguin Group (NZ), 67 Apollo Drive, Rosedale, Auckland 0632, New Zealand
(a division of Pearson New Zealand Ltd)
Penguin Books (South Africa) (Pty) Ltd, Block D, Rosebank Office Park,
181 Jan Smuts Avenue, Parktown North, Gauteng 2193, South Africa

Penguin Books Ltd, Registered Offices: 80 Strand, London WC2R 0RL, England

www.penguin.com

First published in the United States of America by The Viking Press 1962
Published in Penguin Classics 2009

013

Copyright © Shirley Jackson, 1962
Copyright renewed © Barry Hyman, Sarah Webster and Joanne Schnurer, 1990
Introduction copyright © Joyce Carol Oates, 2009

All rights reserved

The moral right of the introducer has been asserted

Printed in England by Clays Ltd, St Ives plc

ISBN: 978-0-141-19145-4

www.greenpenguin.co.uk

MIX
Paper from
responsible sources
FSC
www.fsc.org   FSC™ C018179

Penguin Books is committed to a sustainable
future for our business, our readers and our planet.
This book is made from Forest Stewardship
Council™ certified paper.

For Pascal Covici

My name is Mary Katherine Blackwood. I am eighteen years old, and I live with my sister Constance. I have often thought that with any luck at all I could have been born a werewolf, because the two middle fingers on both my hands are the same length, but I have had to be content with what I had. I dislike washing myself, and dogs, and noise. I like my sister Constance, and Richard Plantagenet, and *Amanita phalloides,* the death-cup mushroom. Everyone else in my family is dead.

The last time I glanced at the library books on the kitchen shelf they were more than five months overdue, and I wondered whether I would have chosen differently if I had known that these were the last books, the ones which would stand forever on our kitchen shelf. We rarely moved things; the Blackwoods were never much of a family for restlessness and stirring. We dealt with the small surface transient objects, the books and the flowers and the spoons, but underneath we had always a solid foundation of stable possessions. We always put things back where they belonged. We dusted and swept under tables and chairs and beds and pictures and rugs and lamps, but we left them where they were; the tortoise-shell toilet set on our mother's dressing table was never off place by so much as a fraction of an inch. Blackwoods had always lived in our house, and kept their things in order; as soon as a new Blackwood wife moved in, a place was found for her belongings, and so our house was built up with layers of Blackwood property weighting it, and keeping it steady against the world.

It was on a Friday in late April that I brought the library books into our house. Fridays and Tuesdays were terrible days, because I had to go into the village. Someone had to go to the library, and the grocery; Constance never went past her own garden, and Uncle Julian could not. Therefore it was not pride that took me into the village twice a week, or even stubbornness, but only the simple need for books and food. It may have been pride that brought me into Stella's for a cup of coffee before I started home; I told myself it was pride and would not avoid going into Stella's no matter how much I wanted to be at home, but I knew, too, that Stella would see me pass if I did not go in, and perhaps think I was afraid, and that thought I could not endure.

"Good morning, Mary Katherine," Stella always said, reaching over to wipe the counter with a damp rag, "how are you today?"

"Very well, thank you."

"And Constance Blackwood, is she well?"

"Very well, thank you."

"And how is *he*?"

"As well as can be expected. Black coffee, please."

If anyone else came in and sat down at the counter I would leave my coffee without seeming hurried, and leave, nodding goodbye to Stella. "Keep well," she always said automatically as I went out.

I chose the library books with care. There were books in our house, of course; our father's study had books covering two walls, but I liked fairy tales and books of history, and Constance liked books about food. Although Uncle Julian never took up a book, he liked to see Constance reading in the evenings while he worked at his papers, and sometimes he turned his head to look at her and nod.

"What are you reading, my dear? A pretty sight, a lady with a book."

"I'm reading something called *The Art of Cooking*, Uncle Julian."

"Admirable."

We never sat quietly for long, of course, with Uncle Julian in the room, but I do not recall that Constance and I have ever opened the library books which are still on our kitchen shelf. It was a fine April morning when I came out of the library; the sun was shining and the false glorious promises of spring were everywhere, showing oddly through the village grime. I remember that I stood on the library steps holding my books and looking for a minute at the soft hinted green in the branches against the sky and wishing, as I always did, that I could walk home across the sky instead of through the village. From the library steps I could cross the street directly and walk on the other side along to the grocery, but that meant that I must pass the general store and the men sitting in front. In this village the men stayed young and did the gossiping and the women aged with grey evil weariness and stood silently waiting for the men to get up and come home. I could leave the library and walk up the street on this side until I was opposite the grocery and then cross; that was preferable, although it took me past the post office and the Rochester house with the piles of rusted tin and the broken automobiles and the empty gas tins and the old mattresses and plumbing fixtures and wash tubs that the Harler family brought home and—I genuinely believe—loved.

The Rochester house was the loveliest in town and had once had a walnut-panelled library and a second-floor ballroom and a profusion of roses along the veranda; our mother had been born there and by rights it should have belonged to Constance. I decided as I always did that it would be safer to go past the post office and the Rochester house, although I disliked seeing the house where our mother was born. This side of the street was generally deserted in the morning, since it was shady, and after I went into the grocery I would in any case have to pass the general store to get home, and passing it going and coming was more than I could bear.

Outside the village, on Hill Road and River Road and Old Mountain, people like the Clarkes and the Carringtons had built new lovely homes. They had to come through the village to get to Hill Road and River Road because the main street of the village was also the main highway across the state, but the Clarke children and the Carrington boys went to private schools and the food in the Hill Road kitchens came from the towns and the city; mail was taken from the village post office by car along the River Road and up to Old Mountain, but the Mountain people mailed their letters in the towns and the River Road people had their hair cut in the city.

I was always puzzled that the people of the village, living in their dirty little houses on the main highway or out on Creek Road, smiled and nodded and waved when the Clarkes and the Carringtons drove by; if Helen Clarke came into Elbert's Grocery to pick up a can of tomato sauce or a pound of coffee her cook had forgotten everyone told her "Good morning," and said the weather was better today. The Clarkes' house is newer but no finer than the Blackwood house. Our father brought home the first piano ever seen in the village. The Carringtons own the paper mill but the Blackwoods own all the land between the highway and the river. The Shepherds of Old Mountain gave the village its town hall, which is white and peaked and set in a green lawn with a cannon in front. There was some talk once of putting in zoning laws in the village and tearing down the shacks on Creek Road and building up the whole village to match the town hall, but no one ever lifted a finger; maybe they thought the Blackwoods might take to attending town meetings if they did. The villagers get their hunting and fishing licenses in the town hall, and once a year the Clarkes and the Carringtons and the Shepherds attend the town meeting and solemnly vote to get the Harler junk yard off Main Street and take away the benches in front of the general store, and each year the villagers gleefully outvote them. Past the town hall, bearing to the left, is Blackwood Road, which is the way home. Blackwood Road goes in a great circle around the Blackwood land and along every inch of Blackwood Road is a wire fence built by our father. Not far past the town hall is the big black rock which marks the entrance to the path where I unlock the gate and lock it behind me and go through the woods and am home.

The people of the village have always hated us.

I played a game when I did the shopping. I thought about the children's games where the board is marked into little spaces and each player moves according to a throw of the dice; there were always dangers, like "lose one turn" and "go back four spaces" and "return to Start," and little helps, like "advance three spaces" and "take an extra turn." The library was my start and the black rock was my goal. I had to move down one side of Main Street, cross, and then move up the other side until I reached the black rock, when I would win. I began well, with a good safe turn along the empty side of Main Street, and perhaps this would turn out to be one of the very good days; it was like that sometimes, but not often on spring mornings. If it was a very good day I would later make an offering of jewelry out of gratitude.

I walked quickly when I started, taking a deep breath to go on with and not looking around; I had the library books and my shopping bag to carry and I watched my feet moving one after the other; two feet in our mother's old brown shoes. I felt someone watching me from inside the post office—we did not accept mail, and we did not have a telephone; both had become unbearable six years before—but I could bear a quick stare from the office; that was old Miss Dutton, who never did her staring out in the open like other folks, but only looked out between blinds or from behind curtains. I never looked at the Rochester house. I could not bear to think of our mother being born there. I wondered sometimes if the Harler people knew that they lived in a house which should have belonged to Constance; there was always so much noise of crashing tinware in their yard that they could not hear me walking. Perhaps the Harlers thought that the unending noise drove away demons, or perhaps they were musical and found it agreeable; perhaps the Harlers lived inside the way they did outside, sitting in old bathtubs and eating their dinner off broken plates set on the skeleton of an old Ford car, rattling cans as they ate, and talking in bellows. A spray of dirt always lay across the sidewalk where the Harlers lived.

Crossing the street (lose one turn) came next, to get to the grocery directly opposite. I always hesitated, vulnerable and exposed, on the side of the road while the traffic went by. Most Main Street traffic was going through, cars and trucks passing through the village because the highway did, so the drivers hardly glanced at me; I could tell a local car by the quick ugly glance from the driver and I wondered, always, what would happen if I stepped down from the curb onto the road; would there be a quick, almost unintended swerve toward me? Just to scare me, perhaps, just to see me jump? And then the laughter, coming from all sides, from behind the blinds in the post office, from the men in front of the general store, from the women peering out of the grocery doorway, all of them watching and gloating, to see Mary Katherine Blackwood scurrying out of the way of a car. I sometimes lost two or even three turns because I waited so carefully for the road to clear in both directions before I crossed.

In the middle of the street I came out of the shade and into the bright, misleading sunshine of April; by July the surface of the road would be soft in the heat and my feet would stick, making the crossing more perilous (Mary Katherine Blackwood, her foot caught in the tar, cringing as a car bore down on her; go back, all the way, and start over), and the buildings would be uglier. All of the village was of a piece, a time, and a style; it was as though the people needed the ugliness of the village, and fed on it. The houses and the stores seemed to have been set up in contemptuous haste to provide shelter for the drab and the unpleasant, and the Rochester house and the Blackwood house and even the town hall had been brought here perhaps accidentally from some far lovely country where people lived with grace. Perhaps the fine houses had been captured—perhaps as punishment for the Rochesters and the Blackwoods and their secret bad hearts?—and were held prisoner in the village; perhaps their slow rot was a sign of the ugliness of the villagers. The row of stores along Main Street was unchangingly grey. The people who owned the stores lived above them, in a row of second-story apartments, and the curtains in the regular line of second-story windows were pale and without life; whatever planned to be colorful lost its heart quickly in the village. The blight on the village never came from the Blackwoods; the villagers belonged here and the village was the only proper place for them.

I always thought about rot when I came toward the row of stores; I thought about burning black painful rot that ate away from inside, hurting dreadfully. I wished it on the village.

I had a shopping list for the grocery; Constance made it out for me every Tuesday and Friday before I left home. The people of the village disliked the fact that we always had plenty of money to pay for whatever we wanted; we had taken our money out of the bank, of course, and I knew they talked about the money hidden in our house, as though it were great heaps of golden coins and Constance and Uncle Julian and I sat in the evenings, our library books forgotten, and played with it, running our hands through it and counting and stacking and tumbling it, jeering and mocking behind locked doors. I imagine that there were plenty of rotting hearts in the village coveting our heaps of golden coins but they were cowards and they were afraid of Blackwoods. When I took my grocery list out of my shopping bag I took out the purse too so that Elbert in the grocery would know that I had brought money and he could not refuse to sell to me.

It never mattered who was in the grocery. I was always served at once; Mr. Elbert or his pale greedy wife always came right away from wherever they were in the store to get me what I wanted. Sometimes, if their older boy was helping out in school vacation, they hurried to make sure that he was not the one who waited on me and once when a little girl—a child strange to the village, of course—came close to me in the grocery Mrs. Elbert pulled her back so roughly that she screamed and then there was a long still minute while everyone waited before Mrs. Elbert took a breath and said, "Anything else?" I always stood perfectly straight and stiff when the children came close, because I was afraid of them. I was afraid that they might touch me and the mothers would come at me like a flock of taloned hawks; that was always the picture I had in my mind—birds descending, striking, gashing with razor claws. Today I had a great many things to buy for Constance, and it was a relief to see that there were no children in the store and not many women; take an extra turn, I thought, and said to Mr. Elbert, "Good morning."

He nodded to me; he could not go entirely without greeting me and yet the women in the store were watching. I turned my back to them, but I could feel them standing behind me, holding

a can or a half-filled bag of cookies or a head of lettuce, not will-
ing to move until I had gone out through the door again and the
wave of talk began and they were swept back into their own
lives. Mrs. Donell was back there somewhere; I had seen her as I
came in, and I wondered as I had before if she came on purpose
when she knew I was coming, because she always tried to say
something; she was one of the few who spoke.

"A roasting chicken," I said to Mr. Elbert, and across the
store his greedy wife opened the refrigerated case and took out
a chicken and began to wrap it. "A small leg of lamb," I said,
"my Uncle Julian always fancies a roasted lamb in the first
spring days." I should not have said it, I knew, and a little gasp
went around the store like a scream. I could make them run like
rabbits, I thought, if I said to them what I really wanted to, but
they would only gather again outside and watch for me there.
"Onions," I said politely to Mr. Elbert, "coffee, bread, flour.
Walnuts," I said, "and sugar; we are very low on sugar." Somewhere behind me there was a little horrified laugh, and Mr.
Elbert glanced past me, briefly, and then to the items he was arranging on the counter. In a minute Mrs. Elbert would bring
my chicken and my meat, wrapped, and set them down by the
other things; I need not turn around until I was ready to go.
"Two quarts of milk," I said. "A half pint of cream, a pound of
butter." The Harrises had stopped delivering dairy goods to us
six years ago and I brought milk and butter home from the grocery now. "And a dozen eggs." Constance had forgotten to put
eggs on the list, but there had been only two at home. "A box
of peanut brittle," I said; Uncle Julian would clatter and crunch
over his papers tonight, and go to bed sticky.

"The Blackwoods always did set a fine table." That was Mrs.
Donell, speaking clearly from somewhere behind me, and
someone giggled and someone else said "Shh." I never turned; it
was enough to feel them all there in back of me without looking
into their flat grey faces with the hating eyes. I wish you were
all dead, I thought, and longed to say it out loud. Constance
said, "Never let them see that you care," and "If you pay any
attention they'll only get worse," and probably it was true, but
I wished they were dead. I would have liked to come into the

grocery some morning and see them all, even the Elberts and the children, lying there crying with the pain and dying. I would then help myself to groceries, I thought, stepping over their bodies, taking whatever I fancied from the shelves, and go home, with perhaps a kick for Mrs. Donell while she lay there. I was never sorry when I had thoughts like this; I only wished they would come true. "It's wrong to hate them," Constance said, "it only weakens *you,*" but I hated them anyway, and wondered why it had been worth while creating them in the first place.

Mr. Elbert put all my groceries together on the counter and waited, looking past me into the distance. "That's all I want to-day," I told him, and without looking at me he wrote the prices on a slip and added, then passed the slip to me so I could make sure he had not cheated me. I always made a point of checking his figures carefully, although he never made a mistake; there were not many things I could do to get back at them, but I did what I could. The groceries filled my shopping bag and another bag besides, but there was no way of getting them home except by carrying them. No one would ever offer to help me, of course, even if I would let them.

Lose two turns. With my library books and my groceries, go-ing slowly, I had to walk down the sidewalk past the general store and into Stella's. I stopped in the doorway of the grocery, feeling around inside myself for some thought to make me safe. Behind me the little stirrings and coughings began. They were getting ready to talk again, and across the width of the store the Elberts were probably rolling their eyes at each other in relief. I froze my face hard. Today I was going to think about taking our lunch out into the garden, and while I kept my eyes open just enough to see where I was walking—our mother's brown shoes going up and down—in my mind I was setting the table with a green cloth and bringing out yellow dishes and strawber-ries in a white bowl. Yellow dishes, I thought, feeling the eyes of the men looking at me as I went by, and Uncle Julian shall have a nice soft egg with toast broken into it, and I will re-member to ask Constance to put a shawl across his shoulders because it is still very early spring. Without looking I could see the grinning and the gesturing; I wished they were all dead and I was walking on their bodies. They rarely spoke directly to me, but only to each other. "That's one of the Blackwood girls," I heard one of them say in a high mocking voice, "one of the Blackwood girls from Blackwood Farm." "Too bad about the Blackwoods," someone else said, just loud enough, "too bad about those poor girls." "Nice farm out there," they said, "nice land to farm. Man could get rich, farming the Blackwood land. If he had a million years and three heads, and didn't care what grew, a man could get rich. Keep their land pretty well locked up, the Blackwoods do." "Man could get rich." "Too bad about the Blackwood girls." "Never can tell what'll grow on Blackwood land."

I am walking on their bodies, I thought, we are having lunch in the garden and Uncle Julian is wearing his shawl. I always held my groceries carefully along here, because one terrible morning I had dropped the shopping bag and the eggs broke and the milk spilled and I gathered up what I could while they shouted, telling myself that whatever I did I would not run away, shovelling cans and boxes and spilled sugar wildly back into the shopping bag, telling myself not to run away.

In front of Stella's there was a crack in the sidewalk that looked like a finger pointing; the crack had always been there. Other landmarks, like the handprint Johnny Harris made in the concrete foundation of the town hall and the Mueller boy's initials on the library porch, had been put in in times that I remembered; I was in the third grade at the school when the town hall was built. But the crack in the sidewalk in front of Stella's had always been there, just as Stella's had always been there. I remember roller-skating across the crack, and being careful not to step on it or it would break our mother's back, and riding a bicycle past here with my hair flying behind; the villagers had not openly disliked us then although our father said they were trash. Our mother told me once that the crack was here when she was a girl in the Rochester house, so it must have been here when she married our father and went to live on Blackwood Farm, and I suppose the crack was there, like a finger pointing, from the time when the village was first put together out of old grey wood and the ugly people with their evil faces were brought from some impossible place and set down in the houses to live.

Stella bought the coffee urn and put in the marble counter with the insurance money when her husband died, but otherwise there had been no change in Stella's since I could remember; Constance and I had come in here to spend pennies after school and every afternoon we picked up the newspaper to take home for our father to read in the evening; we no longer bought newspapers, but Stella still sold them, along with magazines and penny candy and grey postcards of the town hall.

"Good morning, Mary Katherine," Stella said when I sat down at the counter and put my groceries on the floor; I sometimes thought when I wished all the village people dead that I might spare Stella because she was the closest to kind that any of them could be, and the only one who managed to keep hold of any color at all. She was round and pink and when she put on a bright print dress it stayed looking bright for a little while before it merged into the dirty grey of the rest. "How are you today?" she asked.

"Very well, thank you."

"And Constance Blackwood, is she well?"

"Very well, thank you."

"And how is *he*?"

"As well as can be expected. Black coffee, please." I really preferred sugar and cream in my coffee, because it is such bitter stuff, but since I only came here out of pride I needed to accept only the barest minimum for token.

If anyone came into Stella's while I was there I got up and left quietly, but some days I had bad luck. This morning she had only set my coffee down on the counter when there was a shadow against the doorway, and Stella looked up, and said, "Good morning, Jim." She went down to the other end of the counter and waited, expecting him to sit down there so I could leave without being noticed, but it was Jim Donell and I knew at once that today I had bad luck. Some of the people in the village had real faces that I knew and could hate individually; Jim Donell and his wife were among these, because they were deliberate instead of just hating dully and from habit like the others. Most people would have stayed down at the end of the counter where Stella waited, but Jim Donell came right to the end where I was sitting and took the stool next to me, as close to me as he could come because, I knew, he wanted this morning to be bad luck for me.

"They tell me," he said, swinging to sit sideways on his stool and look at me directly, "they tell me you're moving away."

I wished he would not sit so close to me; Stella came toward us on the inside of the counter and I wished she would ask him to move so I could get up and leave without having to struggle around him. "They tell me you're moving away," he said solemnly.

"No," I said, because he was waiting.

"Funny," he said, looking from me to Stella and then back. "I could have swore someone told me you'd be going soon."

"No," I said.

"Coffee, Jim?" Stella asked.

"Who do you think would of started a story like that, Stella? Who do you think would want to tell me they're moving away when they're not doing any such thing?" Stella shook her head at him, but she was trying not to smile. I saw that my hands were tearing at the paper napkin in my lap, ripping off a little corner, and I forced my hands to be still and made a rule for myself: Whenever I saw a tiny scrap of paper I was to remember to be kinder to Uncle Julian.

"Can't ever tell how gossip gets around," Jim Donell said. Perhaps someday soon Jim Donell would die; perhaps there was already a rot growing inside him that was going to kill him. "Did you ever hear anything like the gossip in this town?" he asked Stella.

"Leave her alone, Jim," Stella said.

Uncle Julian was an old man and he was dying, dying regrettably, more surely than Jim Donell and Stella and anyone else. The poor old Uncle Julian was dying and I made a firm rule to be kinder to him. We would have a picnic lunch on the lawn. Constance would bring his shawl and put it over his shoulders, and I would lie on the grass.

"I'm not bothering anybody, Stell. Am I bothering anybody?

I'm just asking Miss Mary Katherine Blackwood here how it happens everyone in town is saying she and her big sister are going to be leaving us soon. Moving away. Going somewheres else to live." He stirred his coffee; from the corner of my eye I could see the spoon going around and around and around, and I wanted to laugh. There was something so simple and silly about the spoon going around while Jim Donell talked; I wondered if he would stop talking if I reached out and took hold of the spoon. Very likely he would, I told myself wisely, very likely he would throw the coffee in my face.

"Going somewheres else," he said sadly.

"Cut it out," Stella said.

I would listen more carefully when Uncle Julian told his story. I was already bringing peanut brittle; that was good.

"Here I was all upset," Jim Donell said, "thinking the town would be losing one of its fine old families. That would be really too bad." He swung the other way around on the stool because someone else was coming through the doorway; I was looking at my hands in my lap and of course would not turn around to see who was coming, but then Jim Donell said "Joe," and I knew it was Dunham, the carpenter; "Joe, you ever hear anything like this? Here all over town they're saying that the Blackwoods are moving away, and now Miss Mary Katherine Blackwood sits right here and speaks up and tells me they're not."

There was a little silence. I knew that Dunham was scowling, looking at Jim Donell and at Stella and at me, thinking over what he had heard, sorting out the words and deciding what each one meant. "That so?" he said at last.

"Listen, you two," Stella said, but Jim Donell went right on, talking with his back to me, and his legs stretched out so I could not get past him and outside. "I was saying to people only this morning it's too bad when the old families go. Although you could rightly say a good number of the Blackwoods are gone already." He laughed, and slapped the counter with his hand. "Gone already," he said again. The spoon in his cup was still, but he was talking on. "A village loses a lot of style when the fine old people go. Anyone would think," he said slowly, "that they wasn't wanted."

"That's right," Dunham said, and he laughed.

"The way they live up in their fine old private estate, with their fences and their private path and their stylish way of living." He always went on until he was tired. When Jim Donell thought of something to say he said it as often and in as many ways as possible, perhaps because he had very few ideas and had to wring each one dry. Besides, each time he repeated himself he thought it was funnier; I knew he might go on like this until he was really sure that no one was listening any more, and I made a rule for myself: Never think anything more than once, and I put my hands quietly in my lap. I am living on the moon, I told myself, I have a little house all by myself on the moon.

"Well," Jim Donell said; he smelled, too. "I can always tell people I used to know the Blackwoods. They never did anything to *me* that I can remember, always perfectly polite to *me*. Not," he said, and laughed, "that I ever got invited to take my dinner with them, nothing like that."

"That's enough right there," Stella said, and her voice was sharp. "You go pick on someone else, Jim Donell."

"Was I picking on anyone? You think I *wanted* to be asked to dinner? You think I'm *crazy?*"

"Me," Dunham said, "I can always tell people I fixed their broken step once and never got paid for it." That was true. Constance had sent me out to tell him that we wouldn't pay carpenter's prices for a raw board nailed crookedly across the step when what he was supposed to do was build it trim and new. When I went out and told him we wouldn't pay he grinned at me and spat, and picked up his hammer and pried the board loose and threw it on the ground. "Do it yourself," he said to me, and got into his truck and drove away. "Never did get paid for it," he said now.

"That must of been an oversight, Joe. You just go right up and speak to Miss Constance Blackwood and she'll see you get what's coming to you. Just if you get invited to dinner, Joe, you just be sure and say no thank you to Miss Blackwood."

Dunham laughed. "Not me," he said. "I fixed their step for them and never did get paid for it."

"Funny," Jim Donell said, "them getting the house fixed up and all, and planning to move away all the time."

"Mary Katherine," Stella said, coming down inside the counter to where I was sitting, "you go along home. Just get up off that stool and go along home. There won't be any peace around here until you go."

"Now, *that's* the truth," Jim Donell said. Stella looked at him, and he moved his legs and let me pass. "You just say the word, Miss Mary Katherine, and we'll all come out and help you pack. Just you say the word, Merricat."

"And you can tell your sister from me—" Dunham started to say, but I hurried, and by the time I got outside all I could hear was the laughter, the two of them and Stella.

I liked my house on the moon, and I put a fireplace in it and a garden outside (what would flourish, growing on the moon? I must ask Constance) and I was going to have lunch outside in my garden on the moon. Things on the moon were very bright, and odd colors; my little house would be blue. I watched my small brown feet go in and out, and let the shopping bag swing a little by my side; I had been to Stella's and now I needed only to pass the town hall, which would be empty except for the people who made out dog licenses and the people who counted traffic fines from the drivers who followed the highway into the village and on through, and the people who sent out notices about water and sewage and garbage and forbade other people to burn leaves or to fish; these would all be buried somewhere deep inside the town hall, working busily together; I had nothing to fear from them unless I fished out of season. I thought of catching scarlet fish in the rivers on the moon and saw that the Harris boys were in their front yard, clamoring and quarrelling with half a dozen other boys. I had not been able to see them until I came past the corner by the town hall, and I could still have turned back and gone the other way, up the main highway to the creek, and then across the creek and home along the other half of the path to our house, but it was late, and I had the groceries, and the creek was nasty to wade in our mother's brown shoes, and I thought, I am living on the moon, and I walked quickly. They saw me at once, and I thought of them rotting away and curling in pain and crying out loud; I wanted them doubled up and crying on the ground in front of me.

"Merricat," they called, "Merricat, Merricat," and moved all together to stand in a line by the fence.

I wondered if their parents taught them, Jim Donell and Dunham and dirty Harris leading regular drills of their children, teaching them with loving care, making sure they pitched their voices right; how else could so many children learn so thoroughly?

Merricat, said Connie, would you like a cup of tea?
Oh no, said Merricat, you'll poison me.
Merricat, said Connie, would you like to go to sleep?
Down in the boneyard ten feet deep!

I was pretending that I did not speak their language; on the moon we spoke a soft, liquid tongue, and sang in the starlight, looking down on the dead dried world; I was almost halfway past the fence.

"Merricat, Merricat!"

"Where's old Connie—home cooking dinner?"

"Would you like a cup of tea?"

It was strange to be inside myself, walking steadily and rigidly past the fence, putting my feet down strongly but without haste that they might have noticed, to be inside and know that they were looking at me; I was hiding very far inside but I could hear them and see them still from one corner of my eye. I wished they were all lying there dead on the ground.

"Down in the boneyard ten feet deep."

"Merricat!"

Once when I was going past, the Harris boys' mother came out onto the porch, perhaps to see what they were all yelling so about. She stood there for a minute watching and listening and I stopped and looked at her, looking into her flat dull eyes and knowing I must not speak to her and knowing I would. "Can't you make them stop?" I asked her that day, wondering if there was anything in this woman I could speak to, if she had ever run joyfully over grass, or had watched flowers, or known delight or love. "Can't you make them stop?"

"Kids," she said, not changing her voice or her look or her air of dull enjoyment, "don't call the lady names."

"Yes, ma," one of the boys said soberly.

"Don't go near no fence. Don't call no lady names."

And I walked on, while they shrieked and shouted and the woman stood on the porch and laughed.

Merricat, said Connie, would you like a cup of tea?
Oh, no, said Merricat, you'll poison me.

Their tongues will burn, I thought, as though they had eaten fire. Their throats will burn when the words come out, and in their bellies they will feel a torment hotter than a thousand fires.

"Goodbye, Merricat," they called as I went by the end of the fence, "don't hurry back."

"Goodbye, Merricat, give our love to Connie."

"Goodbye, Merricat," but I was at the black rock and there was the gate to our path.

2

I had to put down the shopping bag to open the lock on the gate; it was a simple padlock and any child could have broken it, but on the gate was a sign saying PRIVATE NO TRESPASSING and no one could go past that. Our father had put up the signs and the gates and the locks when he closed off the path; before, everyone used the path as a short-cut from the village to the highway four-corners where the bus stopped; it saved them perhaps a quarter of a mile to use our path and walk past our front door. Our mother disliked the sight of anyone who wanted to walking past our front door, and when our father brought her to live in the Blackwood house, one of the first things he had to do was close off the path and fence in the entire Blackwood property, from the highway to the creek. There was another gate at the other end of the path, although I rarely went that way, and that gate too had a padlock and a sign saying PRIVATE NO TRESPASSING. "The highway's built for common people," our mother said, "and my front door is private."

Anyone who came to see us, properly invited, came up the main drive which led straight from the gateposts on the highway up to our front door. When I was small I used to lie in my bedroom at the back of the house and imagine the driveway and the path as a crossroad meeting before our front door, and up and down the driveway went the good people, the clean and rich ones dressed in satin and lace, who came rightfully to visit, and back and forth along the path, sneaking and weaving and sidestepping servilely, went the people from the village. They can't get in, I used to tell myself over and over, lying in my dark room with the trees patterned in shadow on the ceiling, they can't ever get in any more; the path is closed forever. Sometimes I stood inside the fence, hidden by the bushes, and watched people walking on the highway to get from the village to the four corners. As far as I knew, no one from the village had ever tried to use the path since our father locked the gates.

When I had moved the shopping bag inside, I carefully locked the gate again, and tested the padlock to make sure it held. Once the padlock was securely fastened behind me I was safe. The path was dark, because once our father had given up any idea of putting his land to profitable use he had let the trees and bushes and small flowers grow as they chose, and except for one great meadow and the gardens our land was heavily wooded, and no one knew its secret ways but me. When I went along the path, going easily now because I was home, I knew each step and every turn. Constance could put names to all the growing things, but I was content to know them by their way and place of growing, and their unfailing offers of refuge. The only prints on the path were my own, going in and out to the village. Past the turn I might find a mark of Constance's foot, because she sometimes came that far to wait for me, but most of Constance's prints were in the garden and in the house. To-day she had come to the end of the garden, and I saw her as soon as I came around the turn; she was standing with the house behind her, in the sunlight, and I ran to meet her.

"Merricat," she said, smiling at me, "look how far I came today."

"It's too far," I said. "First thing I know you'll be following me into the village."

"I might, at that," she said.

Even though I knew she was teasing me I was chilled, but I laughed. "You wouldn't like it much," I told her. "Here, lazy, take some of these packages. Where's my cat?"

"He went off chasing butterflies because you were late. Did you remember eggs? I forgot to tell you."

"Of course. Let's have lunch on the lawn."

When I was small I thought Constance was a fairy princess. I used to try to draw her picture, with long golden hair and eyes as blue as the crayon could make them, and a bright pink spot on either cheek; the pictures always surprised me, because she *did* look like that; even at the worst time she was pink and white and golden, and nothing had ever seemed to dim the brightness of her. She was the most precious person in my world, always. I followed her across the soft grass, past the flowers she tended, into our house, and Jonas, my cat, came out of the flowers and followed me.

Constance waited inside the tall front door while I came up the steps behind her, and then I put my packages down on the table in the hall and locked the door. We would not use it again until afternoon, because almost all of our life was lived toward the back of the house, on the lawn and the garden where no one else ever came. We left the front of the house turned toward the highway and the village, and went our own ways behind its stern, unwelcoming face. Although we kept the house well, the rooms we used together were the back ones, the kitchen and the back bedrooms and the little warm room off the kitchen where Uncle Julian lived; outside was Constance's chestnut tree and the wide, lovely reach of lawn and Constance's flowers and then, beyond, the vegetable garden Constance tended and, past that, the trees which shaded the creek. When we sat on the back lawn no one could see us from anywhere.

I remembered that I was to be kinder to Uncle Julian when I saw him sitting at his great old desk in the kitchen corner playing with his papers. "Will you let Uncle Julian have peanut brittle?" I asked Constance.

"After his lunch," Constance said. She took the groceries carefully from the bags; food of any kind was precious to Constance, and she always touched foodstuffs with quiet respect. I was not allowed to help; I was not allowed to prepare food, nor was I allowed to gather mushrooms, although I sometimes carried vegetables in from the garden, or apples from the old trees. "We'll have muffins," Constance said, almost singing because she was sorting and putting away the food. "Uncle Julian will have an egg, done soft and buttery, and a muffin and a little pudding."

"Pap," said Uncle Julian.

"Merricat will have something lean and rich and salty."

"Jonas will catch me a mouse," I said to my cat on my knee.

"I'm always so happy when you come home from the village," Constance said; she stopped to look and smile at me. "Partly because you bring home food, of course. But partly because I miss you."

"I'm always happy to get home from the village," I told her.

"Was it very bad?" She touched my cheek quickly with one finger.

"You don't want to know about it."

"Someday I'll go." It was the second time she had spoken of going outside, and I was chilled.

"Constance," Uncle Julian said. He lifted a small scrap of paper from his desk and studied it, frowning. "I do not seem to have any information on whether your father took his cigar in the garden as usual that morning."

"I'm sure he did," Constance said. "That cat's been fishing in the creek," she told me. "He came in all mud." She folded the grocery bag and put it with the others in the drawer, and set the library books on the shelf where they were going to stay forever. Jonas and I were expected to stay in our corner, out of the way, while Constance worked in the kitchen, and it was a joy to watch her, moving beautifully in the sunlight, touching foods so softly. "It's Helen Clarke's day," I said. "Are you frightened?"

She turned to smile at me. "Not a bit," she said. "I'm getting better all the time, I think. And today I'm going to make little rum cakes."

"And Helen Clarke will scream and gobble them."

Even now, Constance and I still saw some small society, visiting acquaintances who drove up the driveway to call. Helen Clarke took her tea with us on Fridays, and Mrs. Shepherd or Mrs. Rice or old Mrs. Crowley stopped by occasionally on a Sunday after church to tell us we would have enjoyed the sermon. They came dutifully, although we never returned their calls, and stayed a proper few minutes and sometimes brought flowers from their gardens, or books, or a song that Constance might care to try over on her harp; they spoke politely and with little runs of laughter, and never failed to invite us to their houses although they knew we would never come. They were civil to Uncle Julian, and patient with his talk, they offered to take us for drives in their cars, they referred to themselves as our friends. Constance and I always spoke well of them to each other, because they believed that their visits brought us pleasure. They never walked on the path. If Constance offered them a cutting from a rosebush, or invited them to see a happy new arrangement of colors, they went into the garden, but they never offered to step beyond their defined areas; they walked along the garden and got into their cars by the front door and drove away down the driveway and out through the big gates. Several times Mr. and Mrs. Carrington had come to see how we were getting along, because Mr. Carrington had been a very good friend of our father's. They never came inside or took any refreshment, but they drove to the front steps and sat in their car and talked for a few minutes. "How are you getting along?" they always asked, looking from Constance to me and back; "how are you managing all by yourselves? Is there anything you need, anything we can do? How are you getting along?" Constance always invited them in, because we had been brought up to believe that it was discourteous to keep guests talking outside, but the Carringtons never came into the house. "I wonder," I said, thinking about them, "whether the Carringtons would bring me a horse if I asked them. I could ride it in the long meadow."

Constance turned and looked at me for a minute, frowning a little. "You will not ask them," she said at last. "We do not ask from anyone. Remember that."

"I was teasing," I said, and she smiled again. "I really only want a winged horse, anyway. We could fly you to the moon and back, my horse and I."

"I remember when you used to want a griffin," she said. "Now, Miss Idleness, run out and set the table."

"They quarrelled hatefully that last night," Uncle Julian said. "I won't have it,' she said, 'I won't stand for it, John Blackwood,' and 'We have no choice,' he said. I listened at the door, of course, but I came too late to hear what they quarrelled about; I suppose it was money."

"They didn't often quarrel," Constance said.

"They were almost invariably civil to one another, Niece, if that is what you mean by not quarrelling; a most unsatisfactory example for the rest of us. My wife and I preferred to shout."

"It hardly seems like six years, sometimes," Constance said. I took the yellow tablecloth and went outside to the lawn to start the table; behind me I heard her saying to Uncle Julian, "Sometimes I feel I would give anything to have them all back again."

When I was a child I used to believe that someday I would grow up and be tall enough to touch the tops of the windows in our mother's drawing room. They were summer windows, because the house was really intended to be only a summer house and our father had only put in a heating system because there was no other house for our family to move to in the winters; by rights we should have had the Rochester house in the village, but that was long lost to us. The windows in the drawing room of our house reached from the floor to the ceiling, and I could never touch the top; our mother used to tell visitors that the light blue silk drapes on the windows had been made up fourteen feet long. There were two tall windows in the drawing room and two tall windows in the dining room across the hall, and from the outside they looked narrow and thin and gave the house a gaunt high look. Inside, however, the drawing room was lovely. Our mother had brought golden-legged chairs from the Rochester house, and her harp was here, and the room shone in reflections from mirrors and sparkling glass. Constance and I only used the room when Helen Clarke came for tea, but we kept it perfectly. Constance stood on a stepladder to wash the tops of the windows, and we dusted the Dresden figurines on the mantel, and with a cloth on the end of a broom I went around the wedding-cake trim at the tops of the walls, staring up into the white fruit and leaves, brushing away at cupids and ribbon knots, dizzy always from looking up and walking backward, and laughing at Constance when she caught me. We polished the floors and mended tiny tears in the rose brocade on the sofas and chairs. There was a golden valance over each high window, and golden scrollwork around the fireplace, and our mother's portrait hung in the drawing room; "I cannot bear to see my lovely room untidy," our mother used to say, and so Constance and I had never been allowed in here, but now we kept it shining and silky.

Our mother had always served tea to her friends from a low table at one side of the fireplace, so that was where Constance always set her table. She sat on the rose sofa with our mother's portrait looking down on her, and I sat in my small chair in the corner and watched. I was allowed to carry cups and saucers and pass sandwiches and cakes, but not to pour tea. I disliked eating anything while people were looking at me, so I had my tea afterwards, in the kitchen. That day, which was the last time Helen Clarke ever came for tea, Constance had set the table as usual, with the lovely thin rose-colored cups our mother had always used, and two silver dishes, one with small sandwiches and one with the very special rum cakes; two rum cakes were waiting for me in the kitchen, in case Helen Clarke ate all of these. Constance sat quietly on the sofa; she never fidgeted, and her hands were neatly in her lap. I waited by the window, watching for Helen Clarke, who was always precisely on time. "Are you frightened?" I asked Constance once, and she said, "No, not at all." Without turning I could hear from her voice that she was quiet.

I saw the car turn into the driveway and then saw that there were two people in it instead of one; "Constance," I said, "she's brought someone else."

Constance was still for a minute, and then she said quite firmly, "I think it will be all right."

I turned to look at her, and she was quiet. "I'll send them away," I said. "She knows better than this."

"No," Constance said. "I really think it will be all right. You watch me."

"But I won't *have* you frightened."

"Sooner or later," she said, "sooner or later I will have to take a first step."

I was chilled. "I want to send them away."

"No," Constance said. "Absolutely not."

The car stopped in front of the house, and I went into the hall to open the front door, which I had unlocked earlier because it was not courteous to unlock the door in a guest's face. When I came onto the porch I saw that it was not quite as bad as I had expected; it was not a stranger Helen Clarke had with her, but little Mrs. Wright, who had come once before and been more frightened than anyone else. She would not be too much for Constance, but Helen Clarke ought not to have brought her without telling me.

"Good afternoon, Mary Katherine," Helen Clarke said, coming around the car and to the steps, "isn't this a lovely spring day? How is dear Constance? I brought Lucille." She was going to handle it brazenly, as though people brought almost-strangers every day to see Constance, and I disliked having to smile at her. "You remember Lucille Wright?" she asked me, and poor little Mrs. Wright said in a small voice that she had so wanted to come again. I held the front door open and they came into the hall. They had not worn coats because it was such a fine day, but Helen Clarke had the common sense to delay a minute anyway; "Tell dear Constance we've come," she said to me, and I knew she was giving me time to tell Constance who was here, so I slipped into the drawing room, where Constance sat quietly, and said, "It's Mrs. Wright, the frightened one."

Constance smiled. "Kind of a weak first step," she said. "It's going to be fine, Merricat."

In the hall Helen Clarke was showing off the staircase to Mrs. Wright, telling the familiar story about the carving and the wood brought from Italy; when I came out of the drawing room she glanced at me and then said, "This staircase is one of the wonders of the county, Mary Katherine. Shame to keep it hidden from the world. Lucille?" They moved into the drawing room.

Constance was perfectly composed. She rose and smiled and said she was glad to see them. Because Helen Clarke was ungraceful by nature, she managed to make the simple act of moving into a room and sitting down a complex ballet for three people; before Constance had quite finished speaking Helen Clarke jostled Mrs. Wright and sent Mrs. Wright sideways like a careening croquet ball off into the far corner of the room where she sat abruptly and clearly without intention upon a small and uncomfortable chair. Helen Clarke made for the sofa where Constance sat, nearly upsetting the tea table, and although there were enough chairs in the room and another sofa, she sat finally uncomfortably close to Constance, who detested having anyone near her but me. "Now," Helen Clarke said, spreading, "it's good to see you again."

"So kind of you to have us," Mrs. Wright said, leaning forward. "Such a lovely staircase."

"You look well, Constance. Have you been working in the garden?"

"I couldn't help it, on a day like this." Constance laughed; she was doing very well. "It's so exciting," she said across to Mrs. Wright. "Perhaps you're a gardener, too? These first bright days are so exciting for a gardener."

She was talking a little too much and a little too fast, but no one noticed it except me.

"I do love a garden," Mrs. Wright said in a little burst. "I do so love a garden."

"How is Julian?" Helen Clarke asked before Mrs. Wright had quite finished speaking. "How is old Julian?"

"Very well, thank you. He is expecting to join us for a cup of tea this afternoon."

"Have you met Julian Blackwood?" Helen Clarke asked Mrs. Wright, and Mrs. Wright, shaking her head, began, "I would love to meet him, of course; I have heard so much—" and stopped.

"He's a touch . . . eccentric," Helen Clarke said, smiling at Constance as though it had been a secret until now. I was thinking that if eccentric meant, as the dictionary said it did, *deviating from regularity,* it was Helen Clarke who was far more eccentric than Uncle Julian, with her awkward movements and her unexpected questions, and her bringing strangers here to tea; Uncle Julian lived smoothly, in a perfectly planned pattern, rounded and sleek. She ought not to call people things they're not, I thought, remembering that I was to be kinder to Uncle Julian.

"Constance, you've always been one of my closest friends," she was saying now, and I wondered at her; she really could not see how Constance withdrew from such words. "I'm going to give you just a word of advice, and remember, it comes from a friend."

I must have known what she was going to say, because I was chilled; all this day had been building up to what Helen Clarke was going to say right now. I sat low in my chair and looked hard at Constance, wanting her to get up and run away, wanting her not to hear what was just about to be said, but Helen Clarke went on, "It's spring, you're young, you're lovely, you have a right to be happy. Come back into the world."

Once, even a month ago when it was still winter, words like that would have made Constance draw back and run away; now, I saw that she was listening and smiling, although she shook her head.

"You've done penance long enough," Helen Clarke said.

"I would so like to give a little luncheon—" Mrs. Wright began.

"You've forgotten the milk; I'll get it." I stood up and spoke directly to Constance and she looked around at me, almost surprised.

"Thank you, dear," she said.

I went out of the drawing room and into the hall and started toward the kitchen; this morning the kitchen had been bright and happy and now, chilled, I saw that it was dreary. Constance had looked as though suddenly, after all this time of refusing and denying, she had come to see that it might be possible, after all, to go outside. I realized now that this was the third time in one day that the subject had been touched, and three times makes it real. I could not breathe; I was tied with wire, and my head was huge and going to explode; I ran to the back door and opened it to breathe. I wanted to run; if I could have run to the end of our land and back I would have been all right, but Constance was alone with them in the drawing room and I had to hurry back. I had to content myself with smashing the milk pitcher which waited on the table; it had been our mother's and I left the pieces on the floor so Constance would see them. I took down the second-best milk pitcher, which did not match the cups; I was allowed to pour milk, so I filled it and took it to the drawing room.

"—do with Mary Katherine?" Constance was saying, and then she turned and smiled at me in the doorway. "Thank you, dear," she said, and glanced at the milk pitcher and at me. "Thank you," she said again, and I put the pitcher down on the tray.

"Not too much at first," Helen Clarke said. "That *would* look odd, I grant you. But a call or two on old friends, perhaps a day in the city shopping—no one would recognize you in the city, you know."

"A little luncheon?" Mrs. Wright said hopefully.

"I'll have to think." Constance made a little, laughing, bewildered gesture, and Helen Clarke nodded.

"You'll need some clothes," she said.

I came from my place in the corner to take a cup of tea from Constance and carry it over to Mrs. Wright, whose hand trembled when she took it. "Thank you, my dear," she said. I could see the tea trembling in the cup; it was only her second visit here, after all.

"Sugar?" I asked her; I couldn't help it, and besides, it was polite.

"Oh, no," she said. "No, thank you. No sugar."

I thought, looking at her, that she had dressed to come here today; Constance and I never wore black but Mrs. Wright had perhaps thought it was appropriate, and today she wore a plain black dress with a necklace of pearls. She had worn black the other time, too, I recalled; always in good taste, I thought, except in our mother's drawing room. I went back to Constance and took up the plate of rum cakes and brought them to Mrs. Wright; that was not kind either, and she should have had the sandwiches first, but I wanted her to be unhappy, dressed in black in our mother's drawing room. "My sister made these this morning," I said.

"Thank you," she said. Her hand hesitated over the plate and then she took a rum cake and set it carefully on the edge of her saucer. I thought that Mrs. Wright was being almost hysterically polite, and I said, "Do take two. Everything my sister cooks is delicious."

"No," she said. "Oh, no. Thank you."

Helen Clarke was eating sandwiches, reaching down past Constance to take one after another. She wouldn't behave like this anywhere else, I thought, only here. She never cares what Constance thinks or I think of her manners; she only supposes we are so very glad to see her. Go away, I told her in my mind. Go away, go away. I wondered if Helen Clarke saved particular costumes for her visits to our house. "This," I could imagine her saying, turning out her closet, "no sense in throwing *this* away, I can keep it for visiting dear Constance." I began dressing Helen Clarke in my mind, putting her in a bathing suit on a snow bank, setting her high in the hard branches of a tree in a dress of flimsy pink ruffles that caught and pulled and tore; she was tangled in the tree and screaming and I almost laughed.

"Why not ask some people here?" Helen Clarke was saying to Constance. "A few old friends—there are many people who have wanted to keep in touch with you, Constance dear—a few old friends some evening. For dinner? No," she said, "perhaps not for dinner. Perhaps not, not at first."

"I myself—" Mrs. Wright began again; she had set her cup of tea and the little rum cake carefully on the table next to her.

"Although why not for dinner?" Helen Clarke said. "After all, you have to take the plunge sometime."

I was going to have to say something. Constance was not looking at me, but only at Helen Clarke. "Why not invite some good people from the village?" I asked loudly.

"Good heavens, Mary Katherine," Helen Clarke said. "You really startled me." She laughed. "I don't recall that the Blackwoods ever mingled socially with the villagers," she said.

"They hate us," I said.

"*I* don't listen to their gossip, and I hope you don't. And, Mary Katherine, you know as well as I do that nine-tenths of that feeling is nothing but your imagination, and if you'd go halfway to be friendly there'd never be a word said against you. Good heavens. I grant you there might have been a little feeling once, but on your side it's just been exaggerated out of all proportion."

"People *will* gossip," Mrs. Wright said reassuringly.

"I've been saying right along that I was a close friend of the Blackwoods and not the least bit ashamed of it, either. You want to come to people of your *own* kind, Constance. They don't talk about *us*."

I wished they would be more amusing; I thought that now Constance was looking a little tired. If they would leave soon I would brush Constance's hair until she fell asleep.

"Uncle Julian is coming," I said to Constance. I could hear the soft sound of the wheel chair in the hall and I got up to open the door.

Helen Clarke said, "Do you suppose that people would really be afraid to visit here?" and Uncle Julian stopped in the doorway. He had put on his dandyish tie for company at tea, and washed his face until it was pink. "Afraid?" he said. "To visit here?" He bowed to Mrs. Wright from his chair and then to Helen Clarke. "Madam," he said, and "Madam." I knew that he could not remember either of their names, or whether he had ever seen them before.

"You look well, Julian," Helen Clarke said.

"Afraid to visit here? I apologize for repeating your words, madam, but I am astonished. My niece, after all, was acquitted of murder. There could be no possible danger in visiting here *now*."

Mrs. Wright made a little convulsive gesture toward her cup of tea and then set her hands firmly in her lap.

"It could be said that there is danger everywhere," Uncle Julian said. "Danger of poison, certainly. My niece can tell you of the most unlikely perils—garden plants more deadly than snakes and simple herbs that slash like knives through the lining of your belly, madam. My niece—"

"Such a lovely garden," Mrs. Wright said earnestly to Constance. "I'm sure I don't know how you do it."

Helen Clarke said firmly, "Now, that's all been forgotten long ago, Julian. No one ever thinks about it any more."

"Regrettable," Uncle Julian said. "A most fascinating case, one of the few genuine mysteries of our time. Of my time, particularly. My life work," he told Mrs. Wright.

"Julian," Helen Clarke said quickly; Mrs. Wright seemed mesmerized. "There is such a thing as good taste, Julian."

"Taste, madam? Have you ever tasted arsenic? I assure you that there is one moment of utter incredulity before the mind can accept—"

A moment ago poor little Mrs. Wright would probably have bitten her tongue out before she mentioned the subject, but now she said, hardly breathing, "You mean you remember?"

"Remember." Uncle Julian sighed, shaking his head happily. "Perhaps," he said with eagerness, "perhaps you are not familiar with the story? Perhaps I might—"

"Julian," Helen Clarke said, "Lucille does not want to hear it. You should be ashamed to ask her."

I thought that Mrs. Wright very much did want to hear it, and I looked at Constance just as she glanced at me; we were both very sober, to suit the subject, but I knew she was as full of merriment as I; it was good to hear Uncle Julian, who was so lonely most of the time.

And poor, poor Mrs. Wright, tempted at last beyond endurance, was not able to hold it back any longer. She blushed deeply, and faltered, but Uncle Julian was a tempter and Mrs. Wright's human discipline could not resist forever. "It happened right in this house," she said like a prayer.

We were all silent, regarding her courteously, and she whispered, "I *do* beg your pardon."

"Naturally, in this house," Constance said. "In the dining room. We were having dinner."

"A family gathering for the evening meal," Uncle Julian said, caressing his words. "Never supposing it was to be our last."

"Arsenic in the sugar," Mrs. Wright said, carried away, hopelessly lost to all decorum.

"I used that sugar." Uncle Julian shook his finger at her. "I used that sugar myself, on my blackberries. Luckily," and he smiled blandly, "fate intervened. Some of us, that day, she led inexorably through the gates of death. Some of us, innocent and unsuspecting, took, unwillingly, that one last step to oblivion. Some of us took very little sugar."

"I never touch berries," Constance said; she looked directly at Mrs. Wright and said soberly, "I rarely take sugar on anything. Even now."

"It counted strongly against her at the trial," Uncle Julian said. "That she used no sugar, I mean. But my niece has never cared for berries. Even as a child it was her custom to refuse berries."

"Please," Helen Clarke said loudly, "it's *outrageous,* it really is; I can't bear to hear it talked about. Constance—Julian—what will Lucille think of you?"

"No, really," Mrs. Wright said, lifting her hands.

"I won't sit here and listen to another word," Helen Clarke said. "Constance must start thinking about the future; this dwelling on the past is not wholesome; the poor darling has suffered enough."

"Well, I miss them all, of course," Constance said. "Things have been much different with all of them gone, but I'm sure I don't think of myself as suffering."

"In some ways," Uncle Julian sailed on, "a piece of extraordinarily good fortune for me. I am a survivor of the most sensational poisoning case of the century. I have all the newspaper clippings. I knew the victims, the accused, intimately, as only a relative living in the very house *could* know them. I have exhaustive notes on all that happened. I have never been well since."

"I said I didn't want to talk about it," Helen Clarke said.

Uncle Julian stopped. He looked at Helen Clarke, and then at Constance. "Didn't it really happen?" he asked after a minute, fingers at his mouth.

"Of course it really happened." Constance smiled at him.

"I have the newspaper clippings," Uncle Julian said uncertainly. "I have my notes," he told Helen Clarke, "I have written down everything."

"It was a terrible thing." Mrs. Wright was leaning forward earnestly and Uncle Julian turned to her.

"Dreadful," he agreed. "Frightful, madam." He maneuvered his wheel chair so his back was to Helen Clarke. "Would you like to view the dining room?" he asked. "The fatal board? I did not give evidence at the trial, you understand; my health was not equal, then or now, to the rude questions of strangers." He gave a little flick of his head in Helen Clarke's direction. "I wanted badly to take the witness stand. I flatter myself that I would not have appeared to disadvantage. But of course she was acquitted after all."

"Certainly she was acquitted," Helen Clarke said vehemently. She reached for her huge pocketbook and took it up onto her lap and felt in it for her gloves. "No one ever thinks about it any more." She caught Mrs. Wright's eye and prepared to rise.

"The dining room . . . ?" Mrs. Wright said timidly. "Just a glance?"

"Madam." Uncle Julian contrived a bow from his wheel chair, and Mrs. Wright hurried to reach the door and open it for him. "Directly across the hall," Uncle Julian said, and she followed. "I admire a decently curious woman, madam; I could see at once that you were devoured with a passion to view the scene of the tragedy; it happened in this very room, and we still have our dinner in here every night."

We could hear him clearly; he was apparently moving around our dining-room table while Mrs. Wright watched him from the doorway. "You will perceive that our table is round. It is over-large now for the pitiful remnant of our family, but we have been reluctant to disturb what is, after all, a monument of sorts; at one time, a picture of this room would have commanded a large price from any of the newspapers. We were a large family once, you recall, a large and happy family. We had small disagreements, of course, we were not all of us overblessed with patience; I might almost say that there were quarrels. Nothing serious; husband and wife, brother and sister, did not always see eye to eye."

"Then why did she—"

"Yes," Uncle Julian said, "that *is* perplexing, is it not? My brother, as head of the family, sat naturally at the head of the table, there, with the windows at his back and the decanter before him. John Blackwood took pride in his table, his family, his position in the world."

"She never even met him," Helen Clarke said. She looked angrily at Constance. "I remember your father well."

Faces fade away out of memory, I thought. I wondered if I would recognize Mrs. Wright if I saw her in the village. I wondered if Mrs. Wright in the village would walk past me, not seeing; perhaps Mrs. Wright was so timid that she never looked up at faces at all. Her cup of tea and her little rum cake still sat on the table, untouched.

"*And* I was a good friend of your mother's, Constance. That's why I feel able to speak to you openly, for your own good. Your mother would have wanted—"

"—my sister-in-law, who was, madam, a delicate woman. You will have noticed her portrait in the drawing room, and the exquisite line of the jawbone under the skin. A woman born for tragedy, perhaps, although inclined to be a little silly. On her right at this table, myself, younger then, and not an invalid; I have only been helpless since that night. Across from me, the boy Thomas—did you know I once had a nephew, that my brother had a son? Certainly, you would have read about him. He was ten years old and possessed many of his father's more forceful traits of character."

"He used the most sugar," Mrs. Wright said.

"Alas," Uncle Julian said. "Then, on either side of my brother, his daughter Constance and my wife Dorothy, who had done me the honor of casting in her lot with mine, although I do not think that she anticipated anything so severe as arsenic on her blackberries. Another child, my niece Mary Katherine, was not at table."

"She was in her room," Mrs. Wright said.

"A great child of twelve, sent to bed without her supper. But she need not concern us."

I laughed, and Constance said to Helen Clarke, "Merricat was always in disgrace. I used to go up the back stairs with a tray of dinner for her after my father had left the dining room. She was a wicked, disobedient child," and she smiled at me.

"An unhealthy environment," Helen Clarke said. "A child should be punished for wrongdoing, but she should be made to feel that she is still loved. *I* would never have tolerated the child's wildness. And now we really *must* . . ." She began to put on her gloves again.

"—spring lamb roasted, with a mint jelly made from Constance's garden mint. Spring potatoes, new peas, a salad, again from Constance's garden. I remember it perfectly, madam. It is still one of my favorite meals. I have also, of course, made very thorough notes of everything about that meal and, in fact, that entire day. You will see at once how the dinner revolves around my niece. It was early summer, her garden was doing well—the weather was lovely that year, I recall; we have not seen such another summer since, or perhaps I am only getting older. We relied upon Constance for various small delicacies which only she could provide; I am of course not referring to arsenic."

"Well, the blackberries were the important part." Mrs. Wright sounded a little hoarse.

"What a mind you have, madam! So precise, so unerring. I can see that you are going to ask me why she should conceivably have used arsenic. My niece is not capable of such subtlety, and her lawyer luckily said so at the trial. Constance can put her hand upon a bewildering array of deadly substances without ever leaving home; she could feed you a sauce of poison hemlock, a member of the parsley family which produces immediate paralysis and death when eaten. She might have made a marmalade of the lovely thornapple or the baneberry, she might have tossed the salad with *Holcus lanatus,* called velvet grass, and rich in hydrocyanic acid. I have notes on all these, madam. Deadly nightshade is a relative of the tomato; would we, any of us, have had the prescience to decline if Constance served it to us, spiced and made into pickle? Or consider just the mushroom family, rich as that is in tradition and deception. We were all fond of mushrooms—my niece makes a mushroom omelette you must taste to believe, madam—and the common death cup—"

"She should not have been doing the cooking," said Mrs. Wright strongly.

"Well, of course, there is the root of our trouble. Certainly she should not have been doing the cooking if her intention was

to destroy all of us with poison; we would have been blindly un-
selfish to encourage her to cook under such circumstances. But
she was acquitted. Not only of the deed, but of the intention."

"What was wrong with Mrs. Blackwood doing her own
cooking?"

"Please." Uncle Julian's voice had a little shudder in it, and I
knew the gesture he was using with it even though he was out of
my sight. He would have raised one hand, fingers spread, and
he would be smiling at her over his fingers; it was a gallant, Uncle Julian, gesture; I had seen him use it with Constance. "I per-
sonally preferred to chance the arsenic," Uncle Julian said.

"We must go home," Helen Clarke said. "I don't know
what's come over Lucille. I *told* her before we came not to mention this subject."

"I am going to put up wild strawberries this year," Constance said to me. "I noticed a considerable patch of them near
the end of the garden."

"It's terribly tactless of her, and she's keeping *me* waiting."

"—the sugar bowl on the sideboard, the heavy silver sugar
bowl. It is a family heirloom; my brother prized it highly. You
will be wondering about that sugar bowl, I imagine. Is it still in
use? you are wondering; has it been cleaned? you may very well
ask; was it thoroughly washed? I can reassure you at once. My
niece Constance washed it before the doctor or the police had
come, and you will allow that it was not a felicitous moment to
wash a sugar bowl. The other dishes used at dinner were still on
the table, but my niece took the sugar bowl to the kitchen, emp-
tied it, and scrubbed it thoroughly with boiling water. It was a
curious act."

"There was a spider in it," Constance said to the teapot. We
used a little rose-covered sugar bowl for the lump sugar for tea.

"—there was a spider in it, she said. That was what she told
the police. That was why she washed it."

"Well," Mrs. Wright said, "it does seem as though she might
have thought of a better reason. Even if it *was* a real spider—I
mean, you don't wash—I mean, you just take the spider *out*."

"What reason would *you* have given, madam?"

"Well, I've never killed anybody, so I don't know—I mean, I

don't know what I'd say. The first thing that came into my head, I suppose. I mean, she must have been upset."

"I assure you the pangs were fearful; you say you have never tasted arsenic? It is not agreeable. I am extremely sorry for all of them. I myself lingered on in great pain for several days; Constance would, I am sure, have demonstrated only the deepest sympathy for me, but by then, of course, she was largely unavailable. They arrested her at once."

Mrs. Wright sounded more forceful, almost unwillingly eager. "I've always thought, ever since we moved up here, that it would be a wonderful chance to meet you people and *really* find out what happened, because of course there's always that one question, the one nobody has ever been able to answer; of course I hardly expected to *talk* to you about it, but look." There was the sound of a dining-room chair being moved; Mrs. Wright had clearly decided to settle down. "First," she said, "she bought the arsenic."

"To kill rats," Constance said to the teapot, and then turned and smiled at me.

"To kill rats," Uncle Julian said. "The only other popular use for arsenic is in taxidermy, and my niece could hardly pretend a working knowledge of that subject."

"She cooked the dinner, she set the table."

"I confess I am surprised at that woman," Helen Clarke said. "She seems such a quiet little body."

"It was Constance who saw them dying around her like flies—I do beg your pardon—and never called a doctor until it was too late. She washed the sugar bowl."

"There was a spider in it," Constance said.

"She told the police those people deserved to die."

"She was excited, madam. Perhaps the remark was misconstrued. My niece is not hard-hearted; besides, she thought at the time that I was among them and although I deserve to die—we all do, do we not?—I hardly think that my niece is the one to point it out."

"She told the police that it was all her fault."

"Now there," Uncle Julian said, "I think she made a mistake. It was certainly true that she thought at first that her cooking had caused all this, but in taking full blame I think that she was over-eager. I would have advised her against any such attitude had I been consulted; it smacks of self-pity."

"But the great, the unanswered question, is *why*? Why did she do it? I mean, unless we agree that Constance was a homicidal maniac—"

"You have met her, madam."

"I have what? Oh, my goodness yes. I completely forgot. I cannot seem to remember that that pretty young girl is actually—well. Your mass murderer must have a reason, Mr. Blackwood, even if it is only some perverted, twisted—oh, dear. She is such a charming girl, your niece; I cannot remember when I have taken to anyone as I have to her. But if she *is* a homicidal maniac—"

"I'm leaving." Helen Clarke stood up and slammed her pocketbook emphatically under her arm. "Lucille," she said, "I am leaving. We have overstayed all limits of decency; it's after five o'clock."

Mrs. Wright scurried out of the dining room, distraught. "I'm so sorry," she said. "We were chatting and I lost track of time. Oh, dear." She ran to her chair to gather up her pocketbook.

"You haven't even touched your tea," I said, wanting to see her blush.

"Thank you," she said; she looked down at her teacup and blushed. "It was delicious."

Uncle Julian stopped his wheel chair in the center of the room and folded his hands happily before him. He looked at Constance and then raised his eyes to gaze on a corner of the ceiling, sober and demure.

"Julian, goodbye," Helen Clarke said shortly. "Constance, I'm sorry we stayed so long; it was inexcusable. Lucille?"

Mrs. Wright looked like a child who knows it is going to be punished, but she had not forgotten her manners. "Thank you," she said to Constance, putting her hand out and then taking it back again quickly. "I had a very nice time. Goodbye," she said to Uncle Julian. They went into the hall and I followed, to lock the door after they had gone. Helen Clarke started the car before poor Mrs. Wright had quite finished getting herself inside, and the last I heard of Mrs. Wright was a little shriek as the car started down the driveway. I was laughing when I came back into the drawing room, and I went over and kissed Constance. "A very nice tea party," I said.

"That *impossible* woman." Constance put her head back against the couch and laughed. "Ill bred, pretentious, stupid. Why she keeps coming I'll never know."

"She wants to reform you." I took up Mrs. Wright's teacup and her rum cake and brought them over to the tea tray. "Poor little Mrs. Wright," I said.

"You were teasing her, Merricat."

"A little bit, maybe. I can't help it when people are frightened; I always want to frighten them more."

"Constance?" Uncle Julian turned his wheel chair to face her. "How was I?"

"Superb, Uncle Julian." Constance stood up and went over to him and touched his old head lightly. "You didn't need your notes at all."

"It really happened?" he asked her.

"It certainly did. I'll take you in to your room and you can look at your newspaper clippings."

"I think not right now. It has been a superlative afternoon, but I think I am a little tired. I will rest till dinner."

Constance pushed the wheel chair down the hall and I followed with the tea tray. I was allowed to carry dirty dishes but not to wash them, so I set the tray on the kitchen table and watched while Constance stacked the dishes by the sink to wash later, swept up the broken milk pitcher on the floor, and took out the potatoes to start for dinner. Finally I had to ask her; the thought had been chilling me all afternoon. "Are you going to do what she said?" I asked her. "What Helen Clarke said?"

She did not pretend not to understand. She stood there looking down at her hands working, and smiled a little. "I don't know," she said.

3

A change was coming, and nobody knew it but me. Constance suspected, perhaps; I noticed that she stood occasionally in her garden and looked not down at the plants she was tending, and not back at our house, but outward, toward the trees which hid the fence, and sometimes she looked long and curiously down the length of the driveway, as though wondering how it would feel to walk along it to the gates. I watched her. On Saturday morning, after Helen Clarke had come to tea, Constance looked at the driveway three times. Uncle Julian was not well on Saturday morning, after tiring himself at tea, and stayed in his bed in his warm room next to the kitchen, looking out of the window beside his pillow, calling now and then to make Constance notice him. Even Jonas was fretful—he was running up a storm, our mother used to say—and could not sleep quietly; all during those days when the change was coming Jonas stayed restless. From a deep sleep he would start suddenly, lifting his head as though listening, and then, on his feet and moving in one quick ripple, he ran up the stairs and across the beds and around through the doors in and out and then down the stairs and across the hall and over the chair in the dining room and around the table and through the kitchen and out into the garden where he would slow, sauntering, and then pause to lick a paw and flick an ear and take a look at the day. At night we could hear him running, feel him cross our feet as we lay in bed, running up a storm.

All the omens spoke of change. I woke up on Saturday morning and thought I heard them calling me; they want me to get up, I thought before I came fully awake and remembered that they were dead; Constance never called me to wake up. When I dressed and came downstairs that morning she was waiting to make my breakfast, and I told her, "I thought I heard them calling me this morning."

"Hurry with your breakfast," she said. "It's another lovely day."

After breakfast on the good mornings when I did not have to go into the village I had my work to do. Always on Wednesday mornings I went around the fence. It was necessary for me to check constantly to be sure that the wires were not broken and the gates were securely locked. I could make the repairs myself, winding the wire back together where it had torn, tightening loose strands, and it was a pleasure to know, every Wednesday morning, that we were safe for another week.

On Sunday mornings I examined my safeguards, the box of silver dollars I had buried by the creek, and the doll buried in the long field, and the book nailed to the tree in the pine woods; so long as they were where I had put them nothing could get in to harm us. I had always buried things, even when I was small; I remember that once I quartered the long field and buried something in each quarter to make the grass grow higher as I grew taller, so I would always be able to hide there. I once buried six blue marbles in the creek bed to make the river beyond run dry. "Here is treasure for you to bury," Constance used to say to me when I was small, giving me a penny, or a bright ribbon; I had buried all my baby teeth as they came out one by one and perhaps someday they would grow as dragons. All our land was enriched with my treasures buried in it, thickly inhabited just below the surface with my marbles and my teeth and my colored stones, all perhaps turned to jewels by now, held together under the ground in a powerful taut web which never loosened, but held fast to guard us.

On Tuesdays and Fridays I went into the village, and on Thursday, which was my most powerful day, I went into the big attic and dressed in their clothes.

Mondays we neatened the house, Constance and I, going into every room with mops and dustcloths, carefully setting the little things back after we had dusted, never altering the perfect line of our mother's tortoise-shell comb. Every spring we washed and polished the house for another year, but on Mondays we neatened; very little dust fell in their rooms, but even that little could not be permitted to stay. Sometimes Constance tried to neaten Uncle Julian's room, but Uncle Julian disliked being disturbed and kept his things in their own places, and Constance had to be content with washing his medicine glasses and changing his bed. I was not allowed in Uncle Julian's room.

On Saturday mornings I helped Constance. I was not allowed to handle knives, but when she worked in the garden I cared for her tools, keeping them bright and clean, and I carried great baskets of flowers, sometimes, or vegetables which Constance picked to make into food. The entire cellar of our house was filled with food. All the Blackwood women had made food and had taken pride in adding to the great supply of food in our cellar. There were jars of jam made by great-grandmothers, with labels in thin pale writing, almost unreadable by now, and pickles made by great-aunts and vegetables put up by our grandmother, and even our mother had left behind her six jars of apple jelly. Constance had worked all her life at adding to the food in the cellar, and her rows and rows of jars were easily the handsomest, and shone among the others. "You bury food the way I bury treasure," I told her sometimes, and she answered me once: "The food comes from the ground and can't be permitted to stay there and rot; *some*thing has to be done with it." All the Blackwood women had taken the food that came from the ground and preserved it, and the deeply colored rows of jellies and pickles and bottled vegetables and fruit, maroon and amber and dark rich green, stood side by side in our cellar and would stand there forever, a poem by the Blackwood women. Each year Constance and Uncle Julian and I had jam or preserve or pickle that Constance had made, but we never touched what belonged to the others; Constance said it would kill us if we ate it.

This Saturday morning I had apricot jam on my toast, and I thought of Constance making it and putting it away carefully for me to eat on some bright morning, never dreaming that a change would be coming before the jar was finished.

"Lazy Merricat," Constance said to me, "stop dreaming over your toast; I want you in the garden on this lovely day."

She was arranging Uncle Julian's tray, putting his hot milk into a jug painted with yellow daisies, and trimming his toast so it would be tiny and hot and square; if anything looked large, or difficult to eat, Uncle Julian would leave it on the plate. Constance always took Uncle Julian's tray in to him in the morning because he slept painfully and sometimes lay awake in the darkness waiting for the first light and the comfort of Constance with his tray. Some nights, when his heart hurt him badly, he might take one more pill than usual, and then lie all morning drowsy and dull, unwilling to sip from his hot milk, but wanting to know that Constance was busy in the kitchen next door to his bedroom, or in the garden where he could see her from his pillow. On his very good mornings she brought him into the kitchen for his breakfast, and he would sit at his old desk in the corner, spilling crumbs among his notes, studying his papers while he ate. "If I am spared," he always said to Constance, "I will write the book myself. If not, see that my notes are entrusted to some worthy cynic who will not be too concerned with the truth."

I wanted to be kinder to Uncle Julian, so this morning I hoped he would enjoy his breakfast and later come out into the garden in his wheel chair and sit in the sun. "Maybe there will be a tulip open today," I said, looking out through the open kitchen door into the bright sunlight.

"Not until tomorrow, I think," said Constance, who always knew. "Wear your boots if you wander today; it will still be quite wet in the woods."

"There's a change coming," I said.

"It's spring, silly," she said, and took up Uncle Julian's tray. "Don't run off while I'm gone; there's work to be done."

She opened Uncle Julian's door and I heard her say good morning to him. When he said good morning back his voice was old and I knew that he was not well. Constance would have to stay near him all day.

"Is your father home yet, child?" he asked her.

"No, not today," Constance said. "Let me get your other pillow. It's a lovely day."

"He's a busy man," Uncle Julian said. "Bring me a pencil, my dear; I want to make a note of that. He's a very busy man."

"Take some hot milk; it will make you warm."

"You're not Dorothy. You're my niece Constance."

"Drink."

"Good morning, Constance."

"Good morning, Uncle Julian."

I decided that I would choose three powerful words, words of strong protection, and so long as these great words were never spoken aloud no change would come. I wrote the first word—*melody*—in the apricot jam on my toast with the handle of a spoon and then put the toast in my mouth and ate it very quickly. I was one-third safe. Constance came out of Uncle Julian's room carrying the tray.

"He's not well this morning," she said. "He left most of his breakfast and he's very tired."

"If I had a winged horse I could fly him to the moon; he would be more comfortable there."

"Later I'll take him out into the sunshine, and perhaps make him a little eggnog."

"Everything's safe on the moon."

She looked at me distantly. "Dandelion greens," she said. "And radishes. I thought of working in the vegetable garden this morning, but I don't want to leave Uncle Julian. I hope that the carrots . . ." She tapped her fingers on the table, thinking. "Rhubarb," she said.

I carried my breakfast dishes over to the sink and set them down; I was deciding on my second magic word, which I thought might very well be *Gloucester*. It was strong, and I thought it would do, although Uncle Julian might take it into his head to say almost anything and no word was truly safe when Uncle Julian was talking.

"Why not make a pie for Uncle Julian?"

Constance smiled. "You mean, why not make a pie for Merricat? Shall I make a rhubarb pie?"

"Jonas and I dislike rhubarb."

"But it has the prettiest colors of all; nothing is so pretty on the shelves as rhubarb jam."

"Make it for the shelves, then. Make me a dandelion pie."

"Silly Merricat," Constance said. She was wearing her blue dress, the sunlight was patterned on the kitchen floor, and color was beginning to show in the garden outside. Jonas sat on the step, washing, and Constance began to sing as she turned to wash the dishes. I was two-thirds safe, with only one magic word to find.

Later Uncle Julian still slept and Constance thought to take five minutes and run down to the vegetable garden to gather what she could; I sat at the kitchen table listening for Uncle Julian so I could call Constance if he awakened, but when she came back he was still quiet. I ate tiny sweet raw carrots while Constance washed the vegetables and put them away. "We will have a spring salad," she said.

"We eat the year away. We eat the spring and the summer and the fall. We wait for something to grow and then we eat it."

"Silly Merricat," Constance said.

At twenty minutes after eleven by the kitchen clock she took off her apron, glanced in at Uncle Julian, and went, as she always did, upstairs to her room to wait until I called her. I went to the front door and unlocked it and opened it just as the doctor's car turned into the drive. He was in a hurry, always, and he stopped his car quickly and ran up the steps; "Good morning, Miss Blackwood," he said, going past me and down the hall, and by the time he had reached the kitchen he had his coat off and was ready to put it over the back of one of the kitchen chairs. He went directly to Uncle Julian's room without a glance at me or at the kitchen, and then when he opened Uncle Julian's door he was suddenly still, and gentle. "Good morning, Mr. Blackwood," he said, his voice easy, "how are things today?"

"Where's the old fool?" Uncle Julian said, as he always did. "Why didn't Jack Mason come?"

Dr. Mason was the one Constance called the night they all died.

"Dr. Mason couldn't make it today," the doctor said, as he always did. "I'm Dr. Levy. I've come to see you instead."

"Rather have Jack Mason."

"I'll do the best I can."

"Always said I'd outlive the old fool." Uncle Julian laughed thinly. "Why are you pretending with me? Jack Mason died three years ago."

"Mr. Blackwood," the doctor said, "it is a pleasure to have you as a patient." He closed the door very quietly. I thought of using *digitalis* as my third magic word, but it was too easy for someone to say, and at last I decided on *Pegasus*. I took a glass from the cabinet, and said the word very distinctly into the glass, then filled it with water and drank. Uncle Julian's door opened, and the doctor stood in the doorway for a minute.

"Remember, now," he said. "And I'll see you next Saturday."

"Quack," Uncle Julian said.

The doctor turned, smiling, and then the smile disappeared and he began to hurry again. He took up his coat and went off down the hall. I followed him and by the time I came to the front door he was already going down the steps. "Goodbye, Miss Blackwood," he said, not looking around, and got into his car and started at once, going faster and faster until he reached the gates and turned onto the highway. I locked the front door and went to the foot of the stairs. "Constance?" I called.

"Coming," she said from upstairs. "Coming, Merricat."

Uncle Julian was better later in the day, and sat out in the warm afternoon sun, hands folded in his lap, half-dreaming. I lay near him on the marble bench our mother had liked to sit on, and Constance knelt in the dirt, both hands buried as though she were growing, kneading the dirt and turning it, touching the plants on their roots.

"It was a fine morning," Uncle Julian said, his voice going on and on, "a fine bright morning, and none of them knew it was their last. She was downstairs first, my niece Constance. I woke up and heard her moving in the kitchen—I slept upstairs then, I could still go upstairs, and I slept with my wife in our room—and I thought, this is a fine morning, never dreaming then that it was their last. Then I heard my nephew—no, it was my brother; my brother came downstairs first after Constance. I heard him whistling. Constance?"

"Yes?"

"What was the tune my brother used to whistle, and always off-key?"

Constance thought, her hands in the ground, and hummed softly, and I shivered.

"Of course. I never had a head for music; I could remember what people looked like and what they said and what they did but I could never remember what they sang. It was my brother who came downstairs after Constance, never caring of course if he woke people with his noise and his whistling, never thinking that perhaps I might still be asleep, although as it happened I was already awake." Uncle Julian sighed, and lifted his head to look curiously, once, around the garden. "He never knew it was his last morning on earth. He might have been quieter, I think, if he did know. I heard him in the kitchen with Constance and I said to my wife—she was awake, too; his noise had awakened her—I said to my wife, you had better get dressed; we live here with my brother and his wife, after all, and we must remember to show them that we are friendly and eager to help out wherever we can; dress and go down to Constance in the kitchen. She did as she was told; our wives always did as they were told, although my sister-in-law lay in bed late that morning; perhaps *she* had a premonition and wanted to take her earthly rest while she could. I heard them all. I heard the boy go downstairs. I thought of dressing; Constance?"

"Yes, Uncle Julian?"

"I could still dress myself in those days, you know, although that *was* the last day. I could still walk around by myself, and dress myself, and feed myself, and I had no pain. I slept well in those days as a strong man should. I was not young, but I was strong and I slept well and I could still dress myself."

"Would you like a rug over your knees?"

"No, my dear, I thank you. You have been a good niece to me, although there are some grounds for supposing you an undutiful daughter. My sister-in-law came downstairs before I did. We had pancakes for breakfast, tiny thin hot pancakes, and my brother had two fried eggs and my wife—although I did not encourage her to eat heavily, since we were living with

my brother—took largely of sausage. Homemade sausage, made
by Constance. Constance?"

"Yes, Uncle Julian?"

"I think if I had known it was her last breakfast I would have
permitted her more sausage. I am surprised, now I think of it,
that no one suspected it was their last morning; they might not
have grudged my wife more sausage *then*. My brother sometimes remarked upon what we ate, my wife and I; he was a just
man, and never stinted his food, so long as we did not take too
much. He watched my wife take sausage that morning, Constance. I saw him watching her. We took little enough from him,
Constance. He had pancakes and fried eggs and sausage but I
felt that he was going to speak to my wife; the boy ate hugely. I
am pleased that the breakfast was particularly good that day."

"I could make you sausage next week, Uncle Julian; I think
homemade sausage would not disagree with you if you had very
little."

"My brother never grudged our food if we did not take too
much. My wife helped to wash the dishes."

"I was very grateful to her."

"She might have done more, I think now. She entertained my
sister-in-law, and she saw to our clothes, and she helped with the
dishes in the mornings, but I believe that my brother thought
that she might have done more. He went off after breakfast to
see a man on business."

"He wanted an arbor built; it was his plan to start a grape
arbor."

"I am sorry about that; we might now be eating jam from our
own grapes. I was always better able to chat after he was gone;
I recall that I entertained the ladies that morning, and we sat
here in the garden. We talked about music; my wife was quite
musical although she had never learned to play. My sister-in-
law had a delicate touch; it was always said of her that she had
a delicate touch, and she played in the evenings usually. Not
that evening, of course. She was not able to play that evening. In
the morning we thought she would play in the evening as usual.
Do you recall that I was very entertaining in the garden that
morning, Constance?"

"I was weeding the vegetables," Constance said. "I could hear you all laughing."

"I was quite entertaining; I am happy for that now." He was quiet for a minute, folding and refolding his hands. I wanted to be kinder to him, but I could not fold his hands for him, and there was nothing I could bring him, so I lay still and listened to him talk. Constance frowned, staring at a leaf, and the shadows moved softly across the lawn.

"The boy was off somewhere," Uncle Julian said at last in his sad old voice. "The boy had gone off somewhere—was he fishing, Constance?"

"He was climbing the chestnut tree."

"I remember. Of course. I remember all of it very clearly, my dear, and I have it all down in my notes. It was the last morning of all and I would not like to forget. He was climbing the chestnut tree, shouting down to us from very high in the tree, and dropping twigs until my sister-in-law spoke sharply to him. She disliked the twigs falling into her hair, and my wife disliked it too, although she would never have been the first to speak. I think my wife was civil to your mother, Constance. I would hate to think not; we lived in my brother's house and ate his food. I know my brother was home for lunch."

"We had a rarebit," Constance said. "I had been working with the vegetables all morning and I had to make something quickly for lunch."

"It was a rarebit we had. I have often wondered why the arsenic was never put into the rarebit. It is an interesting point, and one I shall bring out forcefully in my book. Why was the arsenic not put into the rarebit? They would have lost some hours of life on that last day, but it would all have been over with that much sooner. Constance, if there is one dish you prepare which I strongly dislike, it is a rarebit. I have never cared for rarebit."

"I know, Uncle Julian. I never serve it to you."

"It would have been most suitable for the arsenic. I had a salad instead, I recall. There was an apple pudding for dessert, left over from the night before."

"The sun is going down." Constance rose and brushed the dirt from her hands. "You'll be chilly unless I take you indoors."

"It would have been far more suitable in the rarebit, Constance. Odd that the point was never brought out at the time. Arsenic is tasteless, you know, although I swear a rarebit is not. Where am I going?"

"You are going indoors. You will rest in your room for an hour until your dinner, and after dinner I will play for you, if you like."

"I cannot afford the time, my dear. I have a thousand details to remember and note down, and not a minute to waste. I would hate to lose any small thing from their last day; my book must be complete. I think, on the whole, it was a pleasant day for all of them, and of course it is much better that they never supposed it was to be their last. I think I am chilly, Constance."

"You will be tucked away in your room in a minute."

I came slowly behind them, unwilling to leave the darkening garden; Jonas came after me, moving toward the light in the house. When Jonas and I came inside Constance was just closing the door to Uncle Julian's room, and she smiled at me. "He's practically asleep already," she said softly.

"When I'm as old as Uncle Julian will you take care of me?" I asked her.

"If I'm still around," she said, and I was chilled. I sat in my corner holding Jonas and watched her move quickly and silently around our bright kitchen. In a few minutes she would ask me to set the table for the three of us in the dining room, and then after dinner it would be night and we would sit warmly together in the kitchen where we were guarded by the house and no one from outside could see so much as a light.

4

On Sunday morning the change was one day nearer. I was resolute about not thinking my three magic words and would not let them into my mind, but the air of change was so strong that there was no avoiding it; change lay over the stairs and the kitchen and the garden like fog. I would not forget my magic words; they were MELODY GLOUCESTER PEGASUS, but I refused to let them into my mind. The weather was uneasy on Sunday morning and I thought that perhaps Jonas would succeed after all in running up a storm; the sun shone into the kitchen but there were clouds moving quickly across the sky and a sharp little breeze that came in and out of the kitchen while I had my breakfast.

"Wear your boots if you wander today," Constance told me.

"I don't expect that Uncle Julian will sit outdoors today; it will be far too cool for him."

"Pure spring weather," Constance said, and smiled out at her garden.

"I love you, Constance," I said.

"I love you too, silly Merricat."

"Is Uncle Julian better?"

"I don't think so. He had his tray while you were still asleep, and I thought he seemed very tired. He said he had an extra pill during the night. I think perhaps he is getting worse."

"Are you worried about him?"

"Yes. Very."

"Will he die?"

"Do you know what he said to me this morning?" Constance turned, leaning against the sink, and looked at me with sadness.

"He thought I was Aunt Dorothy, and he held my hand and said, 'It's terrible to be old, and just lie here wondering when it will happen.' He almost frightened me."

"You should have let me take him to the moon," I said.

"I gave him his hot milk and then he remembered who I was."

I thought that Uncle Julian was probably really very happy, with both Constance and Aunt Dorothy to take care of him, and I told myself that long thin things would remind me to be kinder to Uncle Julian; this was to be a day of long thin things, since there had already been a hair in my toothbrush, and a fragment of a string was caught on the side of my chair and I could see a splinter broken off the back step. "Make him a little pudding," I said.

"Perhaps I will." She took out the long thin slicing knife and set it on the sink. "Or a cup of cocoa. And dumplings with his chicken tonight."

"Do you need me?"

"No, my Merricat. Run along, and wear your boots."

The day outside was full of changing light, and Jonas danced in and out of shadows as he followed me. When I ran Jonas ran, and when I stopped and stood still he stopped and glanced at me and then went briskly off in another direction, as though we were not acquainted, and then he sat down and waited for me to run again. We were going to the long field which today looked like an ocean, although I had never seen an ocean; the grass was moving in the breeze and the cloud shadows passed back and forth and the trees in the distance moved. Jonas disappeared into the grass, which was tall enough for me to touch with my hands while I walked, and he made small crooked movements of his own; for a minute the grass would all bend together under the breeze and then there would be a hurrying pattern across it where Jonas was running. I started at one corner and walked diagonally across the long field toward the opposite corner, and in the middle I came directly to the rock covering the spot where the doll was buried; I could always find it although much of my buried treasure was forever lost. The rock was undisturbed and so the doll was safe. I am walking on buried treasure, I thought, with the grass brushing against my hands and nothing around me but the reach of the long field with the grass blowing and the pine woods at the end; behind me was the house, and far off to my left, hidden by trees and almost out of sight, was the wire fence our father had built to keep people out.

When I left the long field I went between the four apple trees we called our orchard, and along the path toward the creek. My box of silver dollars buried by the creek was safe. Near the creek, well hidden, was one of my hiding places, which I had made carefully and used often. I had torn away two or three low bushes and smoothed the ground; all around were more bushes and tree branches, and the entrance was covered by a branch which almost touched the ground. It was not really necessary to be so secret, since no one ever came looking for me here, but I liked to lie inside with Jonas and know that I could never be found. I used leaves and branches for a bed, and Constance had given me a blanket. The trees around and overhead were so thick that it was always dry inside and on Sunday morning I lay there with Jonas, listening to his stories. All cat stories start with the statement: "My mother, who was the first cat, told me this," and I lay with my head close to Jonas and listened. There was no change coming, I thought here, only spring; I was wrong to be so frightened. The days would get warmer, and Uncle Julian would sit in the sun, and Constance would laugh when she worked in the garden, and it would always be the same. Jonas went on and on ("And then we sang! And then we sang!") and the leaves moved overhead and it would always be the same.

I found a nest of baby snakes near the creek and killed them all; I dislike snakes and Constance had never asked me not to. I was on my way back to the house when I found a very bad omen, one of the worst. My book nailed to a tree in the pine woods had fallen down. I decided that the nail had rusted away and the book—it was a little notebook of our father's, where he used to record the names of people who owed him money, and people who ought, he thought, to do favors for him—was useless now as protection. I had wrapped it very thoroughly in heavy paper before nailing it to the tree, but the nail had rusted and it had fallen. I thought I had better destroy it, in case it was now actively bad, and bring something else out to the tree, perhaps a scarf of our mother's, or a glove. It was really too late, although I did not know it then; he was already on his way to the house. By the time I found the book he had probably already left his suitcase in the post office and was asking directions. All Jonas and I knew then was that we were hungry, and we ran together back to the house, and came with the breeze into the kitchen.

"Did you really forget your boots?" Constance said. She tried to frown and then laughed. "Silly Merricat."

"Jonas had no boots. It's a wonderful day."

"Perhaps tomorrow we'll go to gather mushrooms."

"Jonas and I are hungry *today*."

By then he was already walking through the village toward the black rock, with all of them watching him and wondering and whispering as he passed.

It was the last of our slow lovely days, although, as Uncle Julian would have pointed out, we never suspected it then. Constance and I had lunch, giggling and never knowing that while we were happy he was trying the locked gate, and peering down the path, and wandering the woods, shut out for a time by our father's fence. The rain started while we sat in the kitchen, and we left the kitchen door open so we could watch the rain slanting past the doorway and washing the garden; Constance was pleased, the way any good gardener is pleased with rain. "We'll see color out there soon," she said.

"We'll always be here together, won't we, Constance?"

"Don't you ever want to leave here, Merricat?"

"Where could we go?" I asked her. "What place would be better for us than this? Who wants us, outside? The world is full of terrible people."

"I wonder sometimes." She was very serious for a minute, and then she turned and smiled at me. "Don't you worry, my Merricat. Nothing bad will happen."

That must have been just about the minute he found the entrance and started up the driveway, hurrying in the rain, because I had only a minute or two left before I saw him. I might have used that minute or two for so many things: I might have warned Constance, somehow, or I might have thought of a new, safer, magic word, or I might have pushed the table across the kitchen doorway; as it happened, I played with my spoon, and looked at Jonas, and when Constance shivered I said, "I'll get your sweater for you." That was what brought me into the hall as he was coming up the steps. I saw him through the dining-room window and for a minute, chilled, I could not breathe. I knew the front door was locked; I thought of that first. "Constance," I said softly, not moving, "there's one outside. The kitchen door, quickly." I thought she had heard me, because I heard her move in the kitchen, but Uncle Julian had called at that moment, and she went in to him, leaving the heart of our house unguarded. I ran to the front door and leaned against it and heard his steps outside. He knocked, quietly at first and then firmly, and I leaned against the door, feeling the knocks hit at me, knowing how close he was. I knew already that he was one of the bad ones; I had seen his face briefly and he was one of the bad ones, who go around and around the house, trying to get in, looking in the windows, pulling and poking and stealing souvenirs.

He knocked again, and then called out, "Constance? Constance?"

Well, they always knew her name. They knew her name and Uncle Julian's name and how she wore her hair and the color of the three dresses she had to wear in court and how old she was and how she talked and moved and when they could they looked close in her face to see if she was crying. "I want to talk to Constance," he said outside, the way they always did.

It had been a long time since any of them came, but I had not forgotten how they made me feel. At first, they were always there, waiting for Constance, just wanting to see her. "Look," they said, nudging each other and pointing, "there she is, that one, that's the one, Constance." "Doesn't *look* like a murderess, does she?" they told each other; "listen, see if you can get a picture of her when she shows again." "Let's just take some of these flowers," they said comfortably to each other; "get a rock or something out of the garden, we can take it home to show the kids."

"Constance?" he said outside. "Constance?" He knocked again. "I want to talk to Constance," he said, "I have something important to say to her."

They always had something important they wanted to tell Constance, whether they were pushing at the door or yelling outside or calling on the telephone or writing the terrible terrible letters. Sometimes they wanted Julian Blackwood, but they never asked for me. I had been sent to bed without my supper, I had not been allowed in the courtroom, no one had taken my picture. While they were looking at Constance in the courtroom I had been lying on the cot at the orphanage, staring at the ceiling, wishing they were all dead, waiting for Constance to come and take me home.

"Constance, *can* you hear me?" he called outside. "Please listen for just a minute."

I wondered if he could hear me breathing on the inside of the door; I knew what he would do next. First he would back away from the house, sheltering his eyes from the rain, and look up at the windows upstairs, hoping to see a face looking down. Then he would start toward the side of the house, following the walk which was only supposed to be used by Constance and me. When he found the side door, which we never opened, he would knock there, calling Constance. Sometimes they went away when no one answered at either the front door or the side; the ones who were faintly embarrassed at being here at all and wished they had not bothered to come in the first place because there was really nothing to see and they could have saved their time or gone somewhere else—they usually hurried off when they found they were not going to get in to see Constance, but the stubborn ones, the ones I wished would die and lie there dead on the driveway, went around and around the house, trying every door and tapping on the windows. "We got a *right* to see her," they used to shout, "she killed all those people, didn't she?" They drove cars up to the steps and parked there. Most of them locked their cars carefully, making sure all the windows were shut, before they came to pound at the house and

call to Constance. They had picnics on the lawn and took pictures of each other standing in front of the house and let their
dogs run in the garden. They wrote their names on the walls
and on the front door.

"Look," he said outside, "you've *got* to let me in."

I heard him go down the steps and knew he was looking up.
The windows were all locked. The side door was locked. I knew
better than to try to look out through the narrow glass panels
on either side of the door; they always noticed even the slightest
movement, and if I had even barely touched the dining-room
drapes he would have been running at the house, shouting,
"There she is, there she is." I leaned against the front door and
thought about opening it and finding him dead on the driveway.

He was looking up at a blank face of a house looking down
because we always kept the shades drawn on the upstairs windows; he would get no answer there and I had to find Constance a sweater before she shivered any more. It was safe to go
upstairs, but I wanted to be back with Constance while he was
waiting outside, so I ran up the stairs and snatched a sweater
from the chair in Constance's room and ran downstairs and
down the hall into the kitchen and he was sitting at the table in
my chair.

"I had three magic words," I said, holding the sweater.
"Their names were MELODY GLOUCESTER PEGASUS, and we
were safe until they were said out loud."

"Merricat," Constance said; she turned and looked at me,
smiling. "It's our cousin, our cousin Charles Blackwood. I knew
him at once; he looks like Father."

"Well, Mary," he said. He stood up; he was taller now that
he was inside, bigger and bigger as he came closer to me. "Got
a kiss for your cousin Charles?"

Behind him the kitchen door was open wide; he was the first
one who had ever gotten inside and Constance had let him in.
Constance stood up; she knew better than to touch me but she
said "Merricat, Merricat" gently and held out her arms to me. I
was held tight, wound round with wire, I couldn't breathe, and
I had to run. I threw the sweater on the floor and went out the
door and down to the creek where I always went. Jonas found

me after a while and we lay there together, protected from the
rain by the trees crowding overhead, dim and rich in the kind of
knowing, possessive way trees have of pressing closer. I looked
back at the trees and listened to the soft sound of the water.
There was no cousin, no Charles Blackwood, no intruder inside. It was because the book had fallen from the tree; I had
neglected to replace it at once and our wall of safety had cracked.
Tomorrow I would find some powerful thing and nail it to the
tree. I fell asleep listening to Jonas, just as the shadows were
coming down. Sometime during the night Jonas left me to go
hunting, and I woke a little when he came back, pressing against
me to get warm. "Jonas," I said, and he purred comfortably.
When I woke up the early morning mists were wandering lightly
along the creek, curling around my face and touching me. I lay
there laughing, feeling the almost imaginary brush of the mist
across my eyes, and looking up into the trees.

5

When I came into the kitchen, still trailing mist from the creek, Constance was arranging Uncle Julian's breakfast tray. Uncle Julian was clearly feeling well this morning, since Constance was giving him tea instead of hot milk; he must have awakened early and asked for tea. I went to her and put my arms around her and she turned and hugged me.

"Good morning, my Merricat," she said.

"Good morning, my Constance. Is Uncle Julian better today?"

"Much, much better. And the sun is going to shine after yesterday's rain. And I am going to make a chocolate mousse for your dinner, my Merricat."

"I love you, Constance."

"And I love you. Now what will you have for breakfast?"

"Pancakes. Little tiny hot ones. And two fried eggs. Today my winged horse is coming and I am carrying you off to the moon and on the moon we will eat rose petals."

"Some rose petals are poisonous."

"Not on the moon. Is it true that you can plant a leaf?"

"Some leaves. Furred leaves. You can put them in water and they grow roots and then you plant them and they grow into a plant. The kind of a plant they were when they started, of course, not just any plant."

"I'm sorry about that. Good morning, Jonas. You are a furred leaf, I think."

"Silly Merricat."

"I like a leaf that grows into a different plant. All furry."

Constance was laughing. "Uncle Julian will never get his

breakfast if I listen to you," she said. She took up the tray and went into Uncle Julian's room. "Hot tea coming," she said.

"Constance, my dear. A glorious morning, I think. A splendid day to work."

"And to sit in the sun."

Jonas sat in the sunlit doorway, washing his face. I was hungry; perhaps it would be kind to Uncle Julian today if I put a feather on the lawn at the spot where Uncle Julian's chair would go; I was not allowed to bury things in the lawn. On the moon we wore feathers in our hair, and rubies on our hands. On the moon we had gold spoons.

"Perhaps today is a good day to begin a new chapter. Constance?"

"Yes, Uncle Julian?"

"Do you think I should begin chapter forty-four today?"

"Of course."

"Some of the early pages need a little brushing up. A work like this is never done."

"Shall I brush your hair?"

"I think I will brush it myself this morning, thank you. A man's head should be his own responsibility, after all. I have no jam."

"Shall I get you some?"

"No, because I see that I have somehow eaten all my toast. I fancy a broiled liver for my lunch, Constance."

"You shall have it. Shall I take your tray?"

"Yes, thank you. And I will brush my hair."

Constance came back into the kitchen and set down the tray. "And now for you, my Merricat," she said.

"And Jonas."

"Jonas had his breakfast long ago."

"Will you plant a leaf for me?"

"One of these days." She turned her head and listened. "He is still asleep," she said.

"Who is still asleep? Will I watch it grow?"

"Cousin Charles is still asleep," she said, and the day fell apart around me. I saw Jonas in the doorway and Constance by the stove but they had no color. I could not breathe, I was tied around tight, everything was cold.

"He was a ghost," I said.

Constance laughed, and it was a sound very far away. "Then a ghost is sleeping in Father's bed," she said. "And ate a very hearty dinner last night. While you were gone," she said.

"I dreamed that he came. I fell asleep on the ground and dreamed that he came, but then I dreamed him away." I was held tight; when Constance believed me I could breathe again.

"We talked for a long time last night."

"Go and look," I said, not breathing, "go and look; he isn't there."

"Silly Merricat," she said.

I could not run; I had to help Constance. I took my glass and smashed it on the floor. "Now he'll go away," I said.

Constance came to the table and sat down across from me, looking very serious. I wanted to go around the table and hug her, but she still had no color. "My Merricat," she said slowly, "Cousin Charles is here. He *is* our cousin. As long as his father was alive—that was Arthur Blackwood, Father's brother—Cousin Charles could not come to us, or try to help us, because his father would not allow him. His father," she said, and smiled a little, "thought very badly of us. He refused to take care of you during the trial, did you know that? And he never let our names be mentioned in his house."

"Then why do you mention his name in our house?"

"Because I am trying to explain. As soon as his father died Cousin Charles hurried here to help us."

"How can he help us? We're very happy, aren't we, Constance?"

"Very happy, Merricat. But please be pleasant to Cousin Charles."

I could breathe a little; it was going to be all right. Cousin Charles was a ghost, but a ghost that could be driven away. "He'll go away," I said.

"I don't suppose he plans to stay forever," Constance said. "He only came for a visit, after all."

I would have to find something, a device, to use against him. "Has Uncle Julian seen him?"

"Uncle Julian knows he is here, but Uncle Julian was too unwell last night to leave his room. He had his dinner on a tray, only a little soup. I was glad he asked for tea this morning."

"Today we neaten the house."

"Later, after Cousin Charles is awake. And I'd better sweep up that broken glass before he comes down."

I watched her while she swept up the glass; today would be a glittering day, full of tiny sparkling things. There was no point in hurrying with my breakfast, because today I could not go out until we had neatened the house, so I lingered, drinking milk slowly and watching Jonas. Before I was finished Uncle Julian called Constance to come and help him into his chair, and she brought him into the kitchen and put him by his table and his papers.

"I really think I shall commence chapter forty-four," he said, patting his hands together. "I shall commence, I think, with a slight exaggeration and go on from there into an outright lie. Constance, my dear?"

"Yes, Uncle Julian?"

"I am going to say that my wife was beautiful."

Then we were all silent for a minute, puzzled by the sound of a foot stepping upstairs where there had always been silence before. It was unpleasant, this walking overhead. Constance always stepped lightly, and Uncle Julian never walked; this footstep was heavy and even and bad.

"That is Cousin Charles," Constance said, looking up.

"Indeed," said Uncle Julian. He carefully arranged a paper before him and took up a pencil. "I am anticipating considerable pleasure from the society of my brother's son," he said. "Perhaps he can fill in some details on the behavior of his family during the trial. Although, I confess, I have somewhere set down notes on a possible conversation they might have had . . ." He turned to one of his notebooks. "This will delay chapter forty-four, I suspect."

I took Jonas and went to my corner, and Constance went into

the hall to meet Charles when he came down the stairs. "Good morning, Cousin Charles," she said.

"Good morning, Connie." It was the same voice as he had used last night. I got further into my corner as she brought him into the kitchen, and Uncle Julian touched his papers and turned to face the doorway.

"Uncle Julian. I am pleased to meet you at last."

"Charles. You are Arthur's son, but you resemble my brother John, who is dead."

"Arthur's dead, too. That's why I'm here."

"He died wealthy, I trust? I was the only brother with no knack for money."

"As a matter of fact, Uncle Julian, my father left nothing."

"A pity. *His* father left a considerable sum. It came to a considerable sum, even divided among the three of us. I always knew my share would melt away, but I had not suspected it of my brother Arthur. Perhaps your mother was an extravagant woman? I do not remember her very clearly. I recall that when my niece Constance wrote to her uncle during the trial, it was his wife who answered, requesting that the family connection be severed."

"I wanted to come before, Uncle Julian."

"I daresay. Youth is always curious. And a woman of such notoriety as your cousin Constance would present a romantic figure to a young man. Constance?"

"Yes, Uncle Julian?"

"Have I had my breakfast?"

"Yes."

"I will have another cup of tea, then. This young man and I have a great deal to discuss."

I still could not see him clearly, perhaps because he was a ghost, perhaps because he was so very big. His great round face, looking so much like our father's, turned from Constance to Uncle Julian and back, smiling and opening its mouth to talk. I moved as far into my corner as I could, but finally the big face turned at me.

"Why, there's Mary," it said. "Good morning, Mary."

I put my face down to Jonas.

"Shy?" he asked Constance. "Never mind. Kids always take to me."

Constance laughed. "We don't see many strangers," she said. She was not at all awkward or uncomfortable; it was as though she had been expecting all her life that Cousin Charles would come, as though she had planned éxactly what to do and say, almost as though in the house of her life there had always been a room kept for Cousin Charles.

He stood up and came closer to me. "That's a handsome cat," he said. "Does it have a name?"

Jonas and I looked at him and then I thought that Jonas's name might be the safest thing to speak to him first. "Jonas," I said.

"Jonas? Is he your special pet?"

"Yes," I said. We looked at him, Jonas and I, not daring to blink or turn away. The big white face was close, still looking like our father, and the big mouth was smiling.

"We're going to be good friends, you and Jonas and I," he said.

"What will you have for breakfast?" Constance asked him, and she smiled at me because I had told him Jonas's name.

"Whatever you're serving," he said, turning away from me at last.

"Merricat had pancakes."

"Pancakes would be great. A good breakfast in charming company on a beautiful day; what more could I ask?"

"Pancakes," observed Uncle Julian, "are an honored dish in this family, although I rarely take them myself; my health permits only the lightest and daintiest foods. Pancakes were served for breakfast on that last—"

"Uncle Julian," Constance said, "your papers are spilling on the floor."

"Let me get them, sir." Cousin Charles kneeled to gather the papers and Constance said, "After breakfast you'll see my garden."

"A chivalrous young man," Uncle Julian said, accepting his papers from Charles. "I thank you; I am not able myself to leap across a room and kneel on the floor and I am gratified to find someone who can. I believe that you are a year or so older than my niece?"

"I'm thirty-two," Charles said.

"And Constance is approximately twenty-eight. We long ago gave up the practice of birthdays, but twenty-eight should be about right. Constance, I should not be talking so on an empty stomach. Where is my breakfast?"

"You finished it an hour ago, Uncle Julian. I am making you a cup of tea, and pancakes for Cousin Charles."

"Charles is intrepid. Your cooking, although it is of a very high standard indeed, has certain disadvantages."

"I'm not afraid to eat anything Constance cooks," Charles said.

"Really?" said Uncle Julian. "I congratulate you. I was referring to the effect a weighty meal like pancakes is apt to have on a delicate stomach. I suppose *your* reference was to arsenic."

"Come and have your breakfast," Constance said.

I was laughing, although Jonas hid my face. It took Charles a good half-minute to pick up his fork, and he kept smiling at Constance. Finally, knowing that Constance and Uncle Julian and Jonas and I were watching him, he cut off a small piece of pancake and brought it to his mouth, but could not bring himself to put it inside. Finally he set the fork with the piece of pancake down on his plate and turned to Uncle Julian. "You know, I was thinking," he said. "Maybe while I'm here there are things I could do for you—dig in the garden, maybe, or run errands. I'm pretty good at hard work."

"You had dinner here last night and woke up alive this morning," Constance said; I was laughing but she suddenly looked almost cross.

"What?" Charles said. "Oh." He looked down at his fork as though he had forgotten it and at last he picked it up and put the piece of pancake into his mouth very quickly, and chewed it and swallowed it and looked up at Constance. "Delicious," he said, and Constance smiled.

"Constance?"

"Yes, Uncle Julian?"

"I think I shall not, after all, begin chapter forty-four this morning. I think I shall go back to chapter seventeen, where I recall that I made some slight mention of your cousin and his family, and their attitude during the trial. Charles, you are a clever young man. I am eager to hear your story."

"It was all so long ago," Charles said.

"You should have kept notes," Uncle Julian said.

"I mean," Charles said, "can't it all be forgotten? There's no point in keeping those memories alive."

"Forgotten?" Uncle Julian said. "Forgotten?"

"It was a sad and horrible time and it's not going to do Connie here any good at all to keep talking about it."

"Young man, you are speaking slightingly, I believe, of my work. A man does not take his work lightly. A man has his work to do, and he does it. Remember that, Charles."

"I'm just saying that I don't want to talk about Connie and that bad time."

"I shall be forced to invent, to fictionalize, to imagine."

"I refuse to discuss it any further."

"Constance?"

"Yes, Uncle Julian?" Constance looked very serious.

"It *did* happen? I remember that it happened," said Uncle Julian, fingers at his mouth.

Constance hesitated, and then she said, "Of course it did, Uncle Julian."

"My notes . . ." Uncle Julian's voice trailed off, and he gestured at his papers.

"Yes, Uncle Julian. It was real."

I was angry because Charles ought to be kind to Uncle Julian. I remembered that today was to be a day of sparkles and light, and I thought that I would find something bright and pretty to put near Uncle Julian's chair.

"Constance?"

"Yes?"

"May I go outside? Am I warm enough?"

"I think so, Uncle Julian." Constance was sorry, too. Uncle Julian was shaking his head back and forth sadly and he had put down his pencil. Constance went into Uncle Julian's room and brought out his shawl, which she put around his shoulders very gently. Charles was eating his pancakes bravely now, and did not look up; I wondered if he cared that he had not been kind to Uncle Julian.

"Now you will go outside," Constance said quietly to Uncle Julian, "and the sun will be warm and the garden will be bright and you will have broiled liver for your lunch."

"Perhaps not," Uncle Julian said. "Perhaps I had better have just an egg."

Constance wheeled him gently to the door and eased his chair carefully down the step. Charles looked up from his pancakes but when he started to rise to help her she shook her head. "I'll put you in your special corner," she said to Uncle Julian, "where I can see you every minute and five times an hour I'll wave hello to you."

We could hear her talking all the time she was wheeling Uncle Julian to his corner. Jonas left me and went to sit in the doorway and watch them. "Jonas?" Charles said, and Jonas turned toward him. "Cousin Mary doesn't like me," Charles said to Jonas. I disliked the way he was talking to Jonas and I disliked the way Jonas appeared to be listening to him. "How can I make Cousin Mary like me?" Charles said, and Jonas looked quickly at me and then back to Charles. "Here I've come to visit my two dear cousins," Charles said, "my two dear cousins and my old uncle whom I haven't seen for years, and my Cousin Mary won't even be polite to me. What do you think, Jonas?"

There were sparkles at the sink where a drop of water was swelling to fall. Perhaps if I held my breath until the drop fell Charles would go away, but I knew that was not true; holding my breath was too easy.

"Oh, well," Charles said to Jonas, "*Constance* likes me, and I guess that's all that matters."

Constance came to the doorway, waited for Jonas to move, and when he did not, stepped over him. "More pancakes?" she said to Charles.

"No, thanks. I'm trying to get acquainted with my little cousin."

"It won't be long before she's fond of you." Constance was looking at me. Jonas had fallen to washing himself, and I thought at last of what to say.

"Today we neaten the house," I said.

Uncle Julian slept all morning in the garden. Constance went often to the back bedroom windows to look down on him while we worked and stood sometimes, with the dustcloth in her hands, as though she were forgetting to come back and dust our mother's jewel box that held our mother's pearls, and her sapphire ring, and her brooch with diamonds. I looked out the window only once, to see Uncle Julian with his eyes closed and Charles standing nearby. It was ugly to think of Charles walking among the vegetables and under the apple trees and across the lawn where Uncle Julian slept.

"We'll let Father's room go this morning," Constance said, "because Charles is living there." Some time later she said, as though she had been thinking about it, "I wonder if it would be right for me to wear Mother's pearls. I have never worn pearls."

"They've always been in the box," I said. "You'd have to take them out."

"It's not likely that anyone would care," Constance said.

"*I* would care, if you looked more beautiful."

Constance laughed, and said, "I'm silly now. Why should I want to wear pearls?"

"They're better off in the box where they belong."

Charles had closed the door of our father's room so I could not look inside, but I wondered if he had moved our father's things, or put a hat or a handkerchief or a glove on the dresser beside our father's silver brushes. I wondered if he had looked into the closet or into the drawers. Our father's room was in the front of the house, and I wondered if Charles had looked down from the windows and out over the lawn and the long driveway to the road, and wanted to be on that road and away home.

"How long did it take Charles to get here?" I asked Constance.

"Four or five hours, I think," she said. "He came by bus to the village, and had to walk from there."

"Then it will take him four or five hours to get home again?"

"I suppose so. When he goes."

"But first he will have to walk back to the village?"

"Unless you take him on your winged horse."

"I don't have any winged horse," I said.

"Oh, Merricat," Constance said. "Charles is *not* a bad man."

There were sparkles in the mirrors and inside our mother's jewel box the diamonds and the pearls were shining in the darkness. Constance made shadows up and down the hall when she went to the window to look down on Uncle Julian and outside the new leaves moved quickly in the sunlight. Charles had only gotten in because the magic was broken; if I could re-seal the protection around Constance and shut Charles out he would have to leave the house. Every touch he made on the house must be erased.

"Charles is a ghost," I said, and Constance sighed.

I polished the doorknob to our father's room with my dustcloth, and at least one of Charles' touches was gone.

When we had neatened the upstairs rooms we came downstairs together, carrying our dustcloths and the broom and dustpan and mop like a pair of witches walking home. In the drawing room we dusted the golden-legged chairs and the harp, and everything sparkled at us, even the blue dress in the portrait of our mother. I dusted the wedding-cake trim with a cloth on the end of a broom, staggering, and looking up and pretending that the ceiling was the floor and I was sweeping, hovering busily in space looking down at my broom, weightless and flying until the room swung dizzily and I was again on the floor looking up.

"Charles has not yet seen this room," Constance said. "Mother was so proud of it; I ought to have showed it to him right away."

"May I have sandwiches for my lunch? I want to go down to the creek."

"Sooner or later you're going to have to sit at the table with him, Merricat."

"Tonight at dinner. I promise."

We dusted the dining room and the silver tea service and the high wooden backs of the chairs. Constance went every few minutes into the kitchen to look out the back door and check on Uncle Julian, and once I heard her laugh and call, "Watch out for the mud down there," and I knew she was talking to Charles.

"Where did you let Charles sit last night at dinner?" I asked her once.

"In Father's chair," she said, and then, "He has a perfect right to sit there. He's a guest, and he even *looks* like Father."

"Will he sit there tonight?"

"Yes, Merricat."

I dusted our father's chair thoroughly, although it was small use if Charles was to sit there again tonight. I would have to clean all the silverware.

When we had finished neatening the house we came back to the kitchen. Charles was sitting at the kitchen table smoking his pipe and looking at Jonas, who was looking back at him. The pipe smoke was disagreeable in our kitchen, and I disliked having Jonas look at Charles. Constance went on out the back door to get Uncle Julian, and we could hear him say, "Dorothy? I was not asleep, Dorothy."

"Cousin Mary doesn't like me," Charles said again to Jonas. "I wonder if Cousin Mary knows how I get even with people who don't like me? Can I help you with that chair, Constance? Have a nice nap, Uncle?"

Constance made sandwiches for Jonas and me, and we ate them in a tree; I sat in a low fork and Jonas sat on a small branch near me, watching for birds.

"Jonas," I told him, "you are not to listen any more to Cousin Charles," and Jonas regarded me in wide-eyed astonishment, that I should attempt to make decisions for him. "Jonas," I said, "he is a ghost," and Jonas closed his eyes and turned away.

It was important to choose the exact device to drive Charles away. An imperfect magic, or one incorrectly used, might only bring more disaster upon our house. I thought of my mother's jewels, since this was a day of sparkling things, but they might not be strong on a dull day, and Constance would be angry if I took them out of the box where they belonged, when she herself had decided against it. I thought of books, which are always strongly protective, but my father's book had fallen from the tree and let Charles in; books, then, were perhaps powerless against Charles. I lay back against the tree trunk and thought of magic; if Charles had not gone away before three days I would smash the mirror in the hall.

He sat across from me at dinner, in our father's chair, with his big white face blotting out the silver on the sideboard behind him. He watched while Constance cut up Uncle Julian's chicken and put it correctly on the plate, and he watched when Uncle Julian took the first bite and turned it over and over in his mouth.

"Here is a biscuit, Uncle Julian," Constance said. "Eat the soft inside."

Constance had forgotten and put dressing on my salad, but I would not have eaten anyway with that big white face watching. Jonas, who was not allowed chicken, sat on the floor beside my chair.

"Does he always eat with you?" Charles asked once, nodding his head at Uncle Julian.

"When he's well enough," Constance said.

"I wonder how you stand it," Charles said.

"I tell you, John," Uncle Julian said suddenly to Charles, "investments are not what they were when Father made his money. He was a shrewd man, but he never understood that times change."

"Who's he talking to?" Charles asked Constance.

"He thinks you are his brother John."

Charles looked at Uncle Julian for a long minute, and then shook his head and returned to his chicken.

"That was my dead wife's chair on your left, young man," Uncle Julian said. "I well recall the last time she sat there; we—"

"None of that," Charles said, and shook his finger at Uncle Julian; he had been holding his chicken in his hands to eat it, and his finger sparkled with grease. "We're not going to talk about it any more, Uncle."

Constance was pleased with me because I had come to the table and when I looked at her she smiled at me. She knew that I disliked eating when anyone was watching me, and she would save my plate and bring it to me later in the kitchen; she did not remember, I saw, that she had put dressing on my salad.

"Noticed this morning," Charles said, taking up the platter of chicken and looking into it carefully, "that there was a broken step out back. How about I fix it for you one of these days? I might as well earn my keep."

"It would be very kind of you," Constance said. "That step has been a nuisance for a long time."

"And I want to run into the village to get some pipe tobacco, so I can pick up anything you need there."

"But I go to the village on Tuesday," I said, startled.

"You do?" He looked at me across the table, big white face turned directly at me. I was quiet; I remembered that walking to the village was the first step on Charles' way home.

"Merricat, dear, I think if Charles doesn't mind it might be a good idea. I never feel quite comfortable when you're away in the village." Constance laughed. "I'll give you a list, Charles, and the money, and you shall be the grocery boy."

"You keep the money in the house?"

"Of course."

"Doesn't sound very wise."

"It's in Father's safe."

"Even so."

"I assure you, sir," Uncle Julian said, "I made a point of examining the books thoroughly before committing myself. I cannot have been deceived."

"So I'm taking little Cousin Mary's job away from her," Charles said, looking at me again. "You'll have to find something else for her to do, Connie."

I had made sure of what to say to him before I came to the table. "The *Amanita phalloides*," I said to him, "holds three different poisons. There is amanitin, which works slowly and is most potent. There is phalloidin, which acts at once, and there is phallin, which dissolves red corpuscles, although it is the least potent. The first symptoms do not appear until seven to twelve hours after eating, in some cases not before twenty-four or even forty hours. The symptoms begin with violent stomach pains, cold sweat, vomiting—"

"Listen," Charles said. He put down his chicken. "You stop that," he said.

Constance was laughing. "Oh, Merricat," she said, laughing through the words, "you *are* silly. I taught her," she told Charles, "there are mushrooms by the creek and in the fields and I made her learn the deadly ones. Oh, Merricat."

"Death occurs between five and ten days after eating," I said.

"I don't think that's very funny," Charles said.

"Silly Merricat," Constance said.

6

The house was not secure just because Charles had gone out of it and into the village; for one thing, Constance had given him a key to the gates. There had originally been a key for each of us; our father had a key, and our mother, and the keys were kept on a rack beside the kitchen door. When Charles started out for the village Constance gave him a key, perhaps our father's key, and a shopping list, and the money to pay for what he bought.

"You shouldn't keep money in the house like this," he said, holding it tight in his hand for a minute before he reached into a back pocket and took out a wallet. "Women alone like you are, you shouldn't keep money in the house."

I was watching him from my corner of the kitchen but I would not let Jonas come to me while Charles was in the house. "Are you sure you put everything down?" he asked Constance. "Hate to make two trips."

I waited until Charles was well along, perhaps almost to the black rock, and then I said, "He forgot the library books."

Constance looked at me for a minute. "Miss Wickedness," she said. "You wanted him to forget."

"How could he know about the library books? He doesn't belong in this house; he has nothing to do with our books."

"Do you know," Constance said, looking into a pot on the stove, "I think that soon we will be picking lettuce; the weather has stayed so warm."

"On the moon," I said, and then stopped.

"On the moon," Constance said, turning to smile at me, "you have lettuce all year round, perhaps?"

"On the moon we have everything. Lettuce, and pumpkin pie and *Amanita phalloides*. We have cat-furred plants and horses dancing with their wings. All the locks are solid and tight, and there are no ghosts. On the moon Uncle Julian would be well and the sun would shine every day. You would wear our mother's pearls and sing, and the sun would shine all the time."

"I wish I could go to your moon. I wonder if I should start the gingerbread now; it will be cold if Charles is late."

"I'll be here to eat it," I said.

"But Charles said he loved gingerbread."

I was making a little house at the table, out of the library books, standing one across two set on edge. "Old witch," I said, "you have a gingerbread house."

"I do not," Constance said. "I have a lovely house where I live with my sister Merricat."

I laughed at her; she was worrying at the pot on the stove and she had flour on her face. "Maybe he'll never come back," I said.

"He has to; I'm making gingerbread for him."

Since Charles had taken my occupation for Tuesday morning I had nothing to do. I wondered about going down to the creek, but I had no reason to suppose that the creek would even be there, since I never visited it on Tuesday mornings; would the people in the village be waiting for me, glancing from the corners of their eyes to see if I was coming, nudging one another, and then turn in astonishment when they saw Charles? Perhaps the whole village would falter and slow, bewildered at the lack of Miss Mary Katherine Blackwood? I giggled, thinking of Jim Donell and the Harris boys peering anxiously up the road to see if I was coming.

"What's funny?" Constance asked, turning to see.

"I was thinking that you might make a gingerbread man, and I could name him Charles and eat him."

"Oh, Merricat, *please*."

I could tell that Constance was going to be irritable, partly because of me and partly because of the gingerbread, so I thought it wiser to run away. Since it was a free morning, and I was uneasy at going out of doors, it might be a good time to search out a device to use against Charles, and I started up-stairs; the smell of baking gingerbread followed me almost halfway to the top. Charles had left his door open, not wide, but enough for me to get a hand inside.

When I pushed a little the door opened wide and I looked in at our father's room, which now belonged to Charles. Charles had made his bed, I noticed; his mother must have taught him. His suitcase was on a chair, but it was closed; there were things belonging to Charles on the dresser where our father's posses-sions had always been kept; I saw Charles' pipe, and a hand-kerchief, things that Charles had touched and used dirtying our father's room. One drawer of the dresser was a little open, and I thought again of Charles picking over our father's clothes. I walked very softly across the room because I did not want Con-stance to hear me from downstairs, and looked into the open drawer. I thought that Charles would not be pleased to know that I had caught him looking at our father's things, and some-thing from this drawer might be extraordinarily powerful, since it would carry a guilt of Charles. I was not surprised to find that he had been looking at our father's jewelry; inside the drawer was a leather box which held, I knew, a watch and chain made of gold, and cuff links, and a signet ring. I would not touch our mother's jewelry, but Constance had not said anything about our father's jewelry, had not even come into this room to neaten, so I thought I could open the box and take something out. The watch was inside, in a small private box of its own, resting on a satin lining and not ticking, and the watch chain was curled be-side it. I would not touch the ring; the thought of a ring around my finger always made me feel tied tight, because rings had no openings to get out of, but I liked the watch chain, which twisted and wound around my hand when I picked it up. I put the jewelry box carefully back inside the drawer and closed the drawer and went out of the room and closed the door after me, and took the watch chain into my room, where it curled again into a sleeping gold heap on the pillow.

I had intended to bury it, but I was sorry when I thought how long it had been there in the darkness in the box in our father's drawer, and I thought that it had earned a place up high, where it could sparkle in the sunlight, and I decided to nail it to the tree where the book had come down. While Constance made gingerbread in the kitchen, and Uncle Julian slept in his room, and Charles walked in and out of the village stores, I lay on my bed and played with my golden chain.

"That's my brother's gold watch chain," Uncle Julian said, leaning forward curiously. "I thought he was buried in it."

Charles' hand was shaking as he held it out; I could see it shaking against the yellow of the wall behind him. "In a tree," he said, and his voice was shaking too. "I found it nailed to a tree, for God's sake. What kind of a house *is* this?"

"It's not important," Constance said. "Really, Charles, it's not important."

"Not important? Connie, this thing's made of *gold.*"

"But no one wants it."

"One of the links is smashed," Charles said, mourning over the chain. "I could have worn it; what a hell of a way to treat a valuable thing. We could have sold it," he said to Constance.

"But why?"

"I certainly did think he was buried in it," Uncle Julian said. "He was never a man to give things away easily. I suppose he never knew they kept it from him."

"It's worth money," Charles said, explaining carefully to Constance. "This is a gold watch chain, worth possibly a good deal of money. Sensible people don't go around nailing this kind of valuable thing to trees."

"Lunch will be cold if you stand there worrying."

"I'll take it up and put it back in the box where it belongs," Charles said. No one but me noticed that he knew where it had been kept. "Later," he said, looking at me, "we'll find out how it got on the tree."

"Merricat put it there," Constance said. "Please do come to lunch."

"How do you know? About Mary?"

"She always does." Constance smiled at me. "Silly Merricat."

"Does she indeed?" said Charles. He came slowly over to the table, looking at me.

"He was a man very fond of his person," Uncle Julian said. "Given to adorning himself, and not overly clean."

It was quiet in the kitchen; Constance was in Uncle Julian's room, putting him to bed for his afternoon nap. "Where would poor Cousin Mary go if her sister turned her out?" Charles asked Jonas, who listened quietly. "What would poor Cousin Mary do if Constance and Charles didn't love her?"

I cannot think why it seemed to me that I might simply ask Charles to go away. Perhaps I thought that he had to be asked politely just once; perhaps the idea of going away had just not come into his mind and it was necessary to put it there. I decided that asking Charles to go away was the next thing to do, before he was everywhere in the house and could never be eradicated. Already the house smelled of him, of his pipe and his shaving lotion, and the noise of him echoed in the rooms all day long; his pipe was sometimes on the kitchen table and his gloves or his tobacco pouch or his constant boxes of matches were scattered through our rooms. He walked into the village each afternoon and brought back newspapers which he left lying anywhere, even in the kitchen where Constance might see them. A spark from his pipe had left a tiny burn on the rose brocade of a chair in the drawing room; Constance had not yet noticed it and I thought not to tell her because I hoped that the house, injured, would reject him by itself.

"Constance," I asked her on a bright morning; Charles had been in our house for three days then, I thought; "Constance, has he said anything yet about leaving?"

She was increasingly cross with me when I wanted Charles to leave; always before Constance had listened and smiled and only been angry when Jonas and I had been wicked, but now she frowned at me often, as though I somehow looked different to her. "I've told you," she said to me, "I've told you and told you that I won't hear any more silliness about Charles. He is our cousin and he has been invited to visit us and he will probably go when he is ready."

"He makes Uncle Julian sicker."

"He's only trying to keep Uncle Julian from thinking about sad things all the time. And I agree with him. Uncle Julian should be cheerful."

"Why should he be cheerful if he's going to die?"

"I haven't been doing my duty," Constance said.

"I don't know what that means."

"I've been hiding here," Constance said slowly, as though she were not at all sure of the correct order of the words. She stood by the stove in the sunlight with color in her hair and eyes and not smiling, and she said slowly, "I have let Uncle Julian spend all his time living in the past and particularly re-living that one dreadful day. I have let you run wild; how long has it been since you combed your hair?"

I could not allow myself to be angry, and particularly not angry with Constance, but I wished Charles dead. Constance needed guarding more than ever before and if I became angry and looked aside she might very well be lost. I said very cautiously, "On the moon . . ."

"On the moon," Constance said, and laughed unpleasantly. "It's all been my fault," she said. "I didn't realize how wrong I was, letting things go on and on because I wanted to hide. It wasn't fair to you or to Uncle Julian."

"And Charles is also mending the broken step?"

"Uncle Julian should be in a hospital, with nurses to take care of him. And you—" She opened her eyes wide suddenly, as though seeing her old Merricat again, and then she held out her arms to me. "Oh, Merricat," she said, and laughed a little. "Listen to me scolding you; how silly I am."

I went to her and put my arms around her. "I love you, Constance."

"You're a good child, Merricat," she said.

That was when I left her and went outside to talk to Charles. I knew I would dislike talking to Charles, but it was almost too late to ask him politely and I thought I should ask him once. Even the garden had become a strange landscape with Charles' figure in it; I could see him standing under the apple trees and the trees were crooked and shortened beside him. I came out the kitchen door and walked slowly toward him. I was trying to think charitably of him, since I would never be able to speak kindly until I did, but whenever I thought of his big white face grinning at me across the table or watching me whenever I moved I wanted to beat at him until he went away, I wanted to stamp on him after he was dead, and see him lying dead on the grass. So I made my mind charitable toward Charles and came up to him slowly.

"Cousin Charles?" I said, and he turned to look at me. I thought of seeing him dead. "Cousin Charles?"

"Well?"

"I have decided to ask you please to go away."

"All right," he said. "You asked me."

"Please will you go away?"

"No," he said.

I could not think of anything further to say. I saw that he was wearing our father's gold watch chain, even with the crooked link, and I knew without seeing that our father's watch was in his pocket. I thought that tomorrow he would be wearing our father's signet ring, and I wondered if he would make Constance put on our mother's pearls.

"You stay away from Jonas," I said.

"As a matter of fact," he said, "come about a month from now, I wonder who *will* still be here? You," he said, "or me?"

I ran back into the house and straight up to our father's room, where I hammered with a shoe at the mirror over the dresser until it cracked across. Then I went into my room and rested my head on the window sill and slept.

I was remembering these days to be kinder to Uncle Julian. I was sorry because he was spending more and more time in his room, taking both his breakfast and his lunch on a tray and only eating his dinners in the dining room under the despising eye of Charles.

"Can't you feed him or something?" Charles asked Constance. "He's got food all over himself."

"I didn't mean to," Uncle Julian said, looking at Constance.

"Ought to wear a baby bib," Charles said, laughing.

While Charles sat in the kitchen in the mornings eating

hugely of ham and potatoes and fried eggs and hot biscuits and doughnuts and toast, Uncle Julian drowsed in his room over his hot milk and sometimes when he called to Constance, Charles said, "Tell him you're busy; you don't have to go running every time he wets his bed; he just likes being waited on."

I always had my breakfast earlier than Charles on those sunny mornings, and if he came down before I finished I would take my plate out and sit on the grass under the chestnut tree. Once I brought Uncle Julian a new leaf from the chestnut tree and put it on his window sill. I stood outside in the sunlight and looked in at him lying still in the dark room and tried to think of ways I might be kinder. I thought of him lying there alone dreaming old Uncle Julian dreams, and I went into the kitchen and said to Constance, "Will you make Uncle Julian a little soft cake for his lunch?"

"She's too busy now," Charles said with his mouth full. "Your sister works like a slave."

"Will you?" I asked Constance.

"I'm sorry," Constance said. "I have so much to do."

"But Uncle Julian is going to die."

"Constance is too busy," Charles said. "Run along and play."

I followed Charles one afternoon when he went to the village. I stopped by the black rock, because it was not one of my days for going into the village, and watched Charles go down the main street. He stopped and talked for a minute to Stella, who was standing in the sunlight outside her shop, and he bought a paper; when I saw him sit down on the benches with the other men I turned and went back to our house. If I went into the village shopping again Charles would be one of the men who watched me going past. Constance was working in her garden and Uncle Julian slept in his chair in the sun, and when I sat quietly on my bench Constance asked, not looking up at me, "Where have you been, Merricat?"

"Wandering. Where is my cat?"

"I think," Constance said, "that we are going to have to forbid your wandering. It's time you quieted down a little."

"Does 'we' mean you and Charles?"

"Merricat." Constance turned toward me, sitting back against her feet and folding her hands before her. "I never realized until lately how wrong I was to let you and Uncle Julian hide here with me. We should have faced the world and tried to live normal lives; Uncle Julian should have been in a hospital all these years, with good care and nurses to watch him. We should have been living like other people. You should . . ." She stopped, and waved her hands helplessly. "You should have boy friends," she said finally, and then began to laugh because she sounded funny even to herself.

"I have Jonas," I said, and we both laughed and Uncle Julian woke up suddenly and laughed a thin old cackle.

"You are the silliest person I ever saw," I told Constance, and went off to look for Jonas. While I was wandering Charles came back to our house; he brought a newspaper and a bottle of wine for his dinner and our father's scarf which I had used to tie shut the gate, because Charles had a key.

"I could have worn this scarf," he said irritably, and I heard him from the vegetable garden where I had found Jonas sleeping in a tangle of young lettuce plants. "It's an expensive thing, and I like the colors."

"It belonged to Father," Constance said.

"That reminds me," Charles said. "One of these days I'd like to look over the rest of his clothes." He was quiet for a minute; I thought he was probably sitting down on my bench. Then he went on, very lightly. "Also," he said, "while I'm here, I ought to go over your father's papers. There might be something important."

"Not *my* papers," Uncle Julian said. "That young man is not to put a finger on *my* papers."

"I haven't even seen your father's study," Charles said.

"We don't use it. Nothing in there is ever touched."

"Except the safe, of course," Charles said.

"Constance?"

"Yes, Uncle Julian?"

"I want you to have my papers afterwards. No one else is to touch my papers, do you hear me?"

"Yes, Uncle Julian."

I was not allowed to open the safe where Constance kept our father's money. I was allowed to go into the study, but I disliked it and never even touched the doorknob. I hoped Constance would not open the study for Charles; he already had our father's bedroom, after all, and our father's watch and his gold chain and his signet ring. I was thinking that being a demon and a ghost must be very difficult, even for Charles; if he ever forgot, or let his disguise drop for a minute, he would be recognized at once and driven away; he must be extremely careful to use the same voice every time, and present the same face and the same manner without a slip; he must be constantly on guard against betraying himself. I wondered if he would turn back to his true form when he was dead. When it grew cooler and I knew that Constance would be taking Uncle Julian indoors I left Jonas asleep on the lettuce plants and came back into the house. When I came into the kitchen Uncle Julian was poking furiously at the papers on his table, trying to get them into a small heap, and Constance was peeling potatoes. I could hear Charles moving around upstairs, and for a minute the kitchen was warm and glowing and bright.

"Jonas is asleep in the lettuce," I said.

"There is nothing I like more than cat fur in my salad," Constance said amiably.

"It is time that I had a box," Uncle Julian announced. He sat back and looked angrily at his papers. "They must all be put into a box, this very minute. Constance?"

"Yes, Uncle Julian; I can find you a box."

"If I put all my papers in a box and put the box in my room, then that dreadful young man cannot touch them. He *is* a dreadful young man, Constance."

"Really, Uncle Julian, Charles is very kind."

"He is dishonest. His father was dishonest. Both my brothers were dishonest. If he tries to take my papers you must stop him; I cannot permit tampering with my papers and I will not tolerate intrusion. You must tell him this, Constance. He is a bastard."

"Uncle Julian—"

"In a purely metaphorical sense, I assure you. Both my brothers married women of very strong will. That is merely a word used—among men, my dear; I apologize for submitting you to such a word—to categorize an undesirable fellow."

Constance turned without speaking and opened the door which led to the cellar stairs and to the rows and rows of food preserved at the very bottom of our house. She went quietly down the stairs, and we could hear Charles moving upstairs and Constance moving downstairs.

"William of Orange was a bastard," Uncle Julian said to himself; he took up a bit of paper and made a note. Constance came back up the cellar stairs with a box which she brought to Uncle Julian. "Here is a clean box," she said.

"What for?" Uncle Julian asked.

"To put your papers in."

"That young man is not to touch my papers, Constance. I will not have that young man going through my papers."

"This is all my fault," Constance said, turning to me. "He should be in a hospital."

"I will put my papers in that box, Constance, my dear, if you will be kind enough to hand it to me."

"He has a happy time," I said to Constance.

"I should have done everything differently."

"It would certainly not be kind to put Uncle Julian in a hospital."

"But I'll have to if I—" and Constance stopped suddenly, and turned back to the sink and the potatoes. "Shall I put walnuts in the applesauce?" she asked.

I sat very quietly, listening to what she had almost said. Time was running shorter, tightening around our house, crushing me. I thought it might be time to smash the big mirror in the hall, but then Charles' feet were coming heavily down the stairs and through the hall and into the kitchen.

"Well, well, everybody's here," he said. "What's for dinner?"

That evening Constance played for us in the drawing room, the tall curve of her harp making shadows against our mother's portrait and the soft notes falling into the air like petals. She played "Over the Sea to Skye" and "Flow Gently, Sweet Afton" and "I Saw a Lady," and other songs our mother used to play, but I never remember that our mother's fingers touched the strings so lightly with such a breath of melody. Uncle Julian kept himself awake, listening and dreaming, and even Charles did not quite dare to put his feet on the furniture in the drawing room, although the smoke from his pipe drifted against the wedding-cake ceiling and he moved restlessly while Constance played.

"A delicate touch," Uncle Julian said once. "All the Blackwood women had a gifted touch."

Charles stopped by the fireplace to knock his pipe against the grate. "Pretty," he said, taking down one of the Dresden figurines. Constance stopped playing and he turned to look at her. "Valuable?"

"Not particularly," Constance said. "My mother liked them."

Uncle Julian said, "My particular favorite was always 'Bluebells of Scotland'; Constance, my dear, would you—"

"No more now," Charles said. "Now Constance and I want to talk, Uncle. We've got plans to make."

7

Thursday was my most powerful day. It was the right day to settle with Charles. In the morning Constance decided to make spice cookies for dinner; that was too bad, because if any of us had known we could have told her not to bother, that Thursday was going to be the last day. Even Uncle Julian did not suspect, however; he felt a little stronger on Thursday morning and late in the morning Constance brought him into the kitchen which smelled richly of spice cookies and he continued putting his papers into the box. Charles had taken a hammer and found nails and a board and was pounding away mercilessly at the broken step; from the kitchen window I could see that he was doing it very badly and I was pleased; I wished the hammer to pound his thumb. I stayed in the kitchen until I was certain that they would all keep where they were for a while and then I went upstairs and into our father's room, walking softly so Constance would not know I was there. The first thing to do was stop our father's watch which Charles had started. I knew he was not wearing it to mend the broken step because he was not wearing the chain, and I found the watch and the chain and our father's signet ring on our father's dresser with Charles' tobacco pouch and four books of matches. I was not allowed to touch matches but in any case I would not have touched Charles' matches. I took up the watch and listened to it ticking because Charles had started it; I could not turn it all the way back to where it had formerly been because he had kept it going for two or three days, but I twisted the winding knob backward until there was a small complaining crack from the watch and the ticking stopped. When I was sure that he could never start it ticking again I put it back gently where I had found it; one thing, at least, had been released from Charles' spell and I thought that I had at last broken through his tight skin of invulnerability. I need not bother about the chain, which was broken, and I disliked the ring. Eliminating Charles from everything he had touched was almost impossible, but it seemed to me that if I altered our father's room, and perhaps later the kitchen and the drawing room and the study, and even finally the garden, Charles would be lost, shut off from what he recognized, and would have to concede that this was not the house he had come to visit and so would go away. I altered our father's room very quickly, and almost without noise.

During the night I had gone out in the darkness and brought in a large basket filled with pieces of wood and broken sticks and leaves and scraps of glass and metal from the field and the wood. Jonas came back and forth with me, amused at our walking silently while everyone slept. When I altered our father's room I took the books from the desk and blankets from the bed, and I put my glass and metal and wood and sticks and leaves into the empty places. I could not put the things which had been our father's into my own room, so I carried them softly up the stairs to the attic where everything else of theirs was kept. I poured a pitcher of water onto our father's bed; Charles could not sleep there again. The mirror over the dresser was already smashed; it would not reflect Charles. He would not be able to find books or clothes and would be lost in a room of leaves and broken sticks. I tore down the curtains and threw them on the floor; now Charles would have to look outside and see the driveway going away and the road beyond.

I looked at the room with pleasure. A demon-ghost would not easily find himself here. I was back in my own room, lying on the bed and playing with Jonas when I heard Charles down below in the garden shouting to Constance. "This is too much," he was saying, "simply too much."

"What now?" Constance asked; she had come to the kitchen door and I could hear Uncle Julian somewhere below saying, "Tell that young fool to stop his bellowing."

I looked out quickly; the broken step had clearly been too much for Charles because the hammer and the board lay on the ground and the step was still broken; Charles was coming up the path from the creek and he was carrying something; I wondered what he had found now.

"Did you ever hear of anything like this?" he was saying; even though he was close now he was still shouting. "Look at this, Connie, just *look* at it."

"I suppose it belongs to Merricat," Constance said.

"It does *not* belong to Merricat, or anything like it. This is *money*."

"I remember," Constance said. "Silver dollars. I remember when she buried them."

"There must be twenty or thirty dollars here; this is outrageous."

"She likes to bury things."

Charles was still shouting, shaking my box of silver dollars back and forth violently. I wondered if he would drop it; I would like to have seen Charles on the ground, scrabbling after my silver dollars.

"It's not her money," he was shouting, "she has no right to hide it."

I wondered how he had happened to find the box where I had buried it; perhaps Charles and money found each other no matter how far apart they were, or perhaps Charles was engaged in systematically digging up every inch of our land. "This is terrible," he was shouting, "terrible; she has no right."

"No harm is done," Constance said. I could see that she was puzzled and somewhere inside the kitchen Uncle Julian was pounding and calling her.

"How do you know there isn't more?" Charles held the box out accusingly. "How do you know that crazy kid hasn't buried thousands of dollars all over, where we'll *never* find it?"

"She likes to bury things," Constance said. "Coming, Uncle Julian."

Charles followed her inside, still holding the box tenderly. I supposed I could bury the box again after he had gone, but I was not pleased. I came to the top of the stairs and watched Charles proceeding down the hall to the study; he was clearly going to put my silver dollars into our father's safe. I ran down the stairs quickly and quietly and out through the kitchen. "Silly Merricat," Constance said to me as I passed; she was putting spice cookies in long rows to cool.

I was thinking of Charles. I could turn him into a fly and drop him into a spider's web and watch him tangled and helpless and struggling, shut into the body of a dying buzzing fly; I could wish him dead until he died. I could fasten him to a tree and keep him there until he grew into the trunk and bark grew over his mouth. I could bury him in the hole where my box of silver dollars had been so safe until he came; if he was under the ground I could walk over him stamping my feet.

He had not even bothered to fill in the hole. I could imagine him walking here and noticing the spot where the ground was disturbed, stopping to poke in it and then digging wildly with both his hands, scowling and finally greedy and shocked and gasping when he found my box of silver dollars. "Don't blame *me*," I said to the hole; I would have to find something else to bury here and I wished it could be Charles.

The hole would hold his head nicely. I laughed when I found a round stone the right size, and scratched a face on it and buried it in the hole. "Goodbye, Charles," I said. "Next time don't go around taking other people's things."

I stayed by the creek for an hour or so; I was staying by the creek when Charles finally went upstairs and into the room which was no longer his and no longer our father's. I thought for one minute that Charles had been in my shelter, but nothing was disturbed, as it would have been if Charles had come scratching around. He had been near enough to bother me, however, so I cleared out the grass and leaves I usually slept on, and shook out my blanket, and put in everything fresh. I washed the flat rock where I sometimes ate my meals, and put a better branch across the entrance. I wondered if Charles would come back looking for more silver dollars and I wondered if he would like my six blue marbles. I was finally hungry and went back to our house, and there in the kitchen was Charles, still shouting.

"I can't *believe* it," he was saying, quite shrill by now, "I simply can't *believe* it."

I wondered how long Charles was going to go on shouting. He made a black noise in our house and his voice was getting thinner and higher; perhaps if he shouted long enough he would squeak. I sat on the kitchen step next to Jonas and thought that perhaps Constance might laugh out loud if Charles squeaked at her. It never happened, however, because as soon as he saw that I was sitting on the step he was quiet for a minute and then when he spoke he had brought his voice down and made it slow.

"So you're back," he said. He did not move toward me but I felt his voice as though he were coming closer. I did not look at him; I looked at Jonas, who was looking at him.

"I haven't quite decided what I'm going to do with you," he said. "But whatever I do, you'll remember it."

"Don't bully her, Charles," Constance said. I did not like her voice either because it was strange and I knew she was uncertain. "It's all my fault, anyway." That was her new way of thinking.

I thought I would help Constance, perhaps make her laugh. "*Amanita pantherina,*" I said, "highly poisonous. *Amanita rubescens,* edible and good. The *Cicuta maculata* is the water hemlock, one of the most poisonous of wild plants if taken internally. The *Apocynum cannabinum* is not a poisonous plant of the first importance, but the snakeberry—"

"Stop it," Charles said, still quiet.

"Constance," I said, "we came home for lunch, Jonas and I."

"First you will have to explain to Cousin Charles," Constance said, and I was chilled.

Charles was sitting at the kitchen table, with his chair pushed back and turned a little to face me in the doorway. Constance stood behind him, leaning against the sink. Uncle Julian sat at his table, stirring papers. There were rows and rows of spice cookies cooling and the kitchen still smelled of cinnamon and nutmeg. I wondered if Constance would give Jonas a spice cookie with his supper but of course she never did because that was the last day.

"Now listen," Charles said. He had brought down a handful of sticks and dirt, perhaps to prove to Constance that they had really been in his room, or perhaps because he was going to clean it away handful by handful; the sticks and dirt looked wrong on the kitchen table and I thought that perhaps one reason Constance looked so sad was the dirt on her clean table. "Now listen," Charles said.

"I cannot work in here if that young man is going to talk all the time," Uncle Julian said. "Constance, tell him he must be quiet for a little while."

"You, too," Charles said in that soft voice. "I have put up with enough from both of you. One of you fouls my room and goes around burying money and the other one can't even remember my name."

"Charles," I said to Jonas. I was the one who buried money, certainly, so I was not the one who could not remember his name; poor old Uncle Julian could not bury anything and could not remember Charles' name. I would remember to be kinder to Uncle Julian. "Will you give Uncle Julian a spice cookie for his dinner?" I asked Constance. "And Jonas one too?"

"Mary Katherine," Charles said, "I am going to give you one chance to explain. Why did you make that mess in my room?"

There was no reason to answer him. He was not Constance, and anything I said to him might perhaps help him to get back his thin grasp on our house. I sat on the doorstep and played with Jonas's ears, which flicked and snapped when I tickled them.

"Answer me," Charles said.

"How often must I tell you, John, that I know nothing whatsoever about it?" Uncle Julian slammed his hand down onto his papers and scattered them. "It is a quarrel between the women and none of my affair. I do not involve myself in my wife's petty squabbles and I strongly advise you to do the same. It is not fitting for men of dignity to threaten and reproach because women have had a falling out. You lose stature, John, you lose stature."

"Shut up," Charles said; he was shouting again and I was pleased. "Constance," he said, lowering his voice a little, "this is terrible. The sooner you're out of it the better."

"—will not be told to shut up by my own brother. We will leave your house, John, if that is really your desire. I ask you, however, to reflect. My wife and I—"

"It's my fault, all of it," Constance said. I thought she was going to cry. It was unthinkable for Constance to cry again after all these years, but I was held tight, I was chilled, and I could not move to go over to her.

"You are evil," I said to Charles. "You are a ghost and a demon."

"What the *hell*?" Charles said.

"Don't pay any attention," Constance told him. "Don't listen to Merricat's nonsense."

"You are a very selfish man, John, perhaps even a scoundrel, and overly fond of the world's goods; I sometimes wonder, John, if you are every bit the gentleman."

"It's a crazy house," Charles said with conviction. "Constance, this is a crazy house."

"I'll clean your room, right away. Charles, please don't be angry." Constance looked at me wildly, but I was held tight and could not see her.

"Uncle Julian." Charles got up and went over to where Uncle Julian sat at his table.

"Don't you touch my papers," Uncle Julian said, trying to cover them with his hands. "You get away from my papers, you bastard."

"What?" said Charles.

"I apologize," Uncle Julian said to Constance. "Not language fitting for your ears, my dear. Just tell this young bastard to stay away from my papers."

"Look," Charles said to Uncle Julian, "I tell you I've had enough of this. I am not going to touch your silly papers and I am not your brother John."

"Of course you are not my brother John; you are not tall enough by half an inch. You are a young bastard and I desire that you return to your father, who, to my shame, is my brother Arthur, and tell him I said so. In the presence of your mother, if you choose; she is a strong-willed woman but lacks family feeling. She desired that the family connection be severed. I have consequently no objection to your repeating my high language in her presence."

"That has all been forgotten, Uncle Julian; Constance and I—"

"I think you have forgotten *yourself*, young man, to take such a tone to me. I am pleased that you are repentant, but you have taken far too much of my time. Please be extremely quiet now."

"Not until I have finished with your niece Mary Katherine."

"My niece Mary Katherine has been a long time dead, young man. She did not survive the loss of her family; I supposed you knew that."

"What?" Charles turned furiously to Constance.

"My niece Mary Katherine died in an orphanage, of neglect, during her sister's trial for murder. But she is of very little consequence to my book, and so we will have done with her."

"She is sitting right here." Charles waved his hands, and his face was red.

"Young man." Uncle Julian put down his pencil and half-turned to face Charles. "I have pointed out to you, I believe, the importance of my work. You choose constantly to interrupt me. I have had enough. You must either be quiet or you must leave this room."

I was laughing at Charles and even Constance was smiling. Charles stood staring at Uncle Julian, and Uncle Julian, going through his papers, said to himself, "Damned impertinent puppy," and then, "Constance?"

"Yes, Uncle Julian?"

"Why have my papers been put into this box? I shall have to take them all out again and rearrange them. Has that young man been near my papers? Has he?"

"No, Uncle Julian."

"He takes a great deal upon himself, I think. When is he going away?"

"I'm not going away," Charles said. "I am going to stay."

"Impossible," Uncle Julian said. "We have not the room. Constance?"

"Yes, Uncle Julian?"

"I would like a chop for my lunch. A nice little chop, neatly broiled. Perhaps a mushroom."

"Yes," Constance said with relief, "I should start lunch." As though she were happy to be doing it at last she came to the table to brush away the dirt and leaves that Charles had left there. She brushed them into a paper bag and threw the bag into the wastebasket, and then she came back with a cloth and scrubbed the table. Charles looked at her and at me and at Uncle Julian. He was clearly baffled, unable to grasp his fingers tightly around anything he saw or heard; it was a joyful sight, to see the first twistings and turnings of the demon caught, and I was very proud of Uncle Julian. Constance smiled down at Charles, happy that no one was shouting any more; she was not going to cry now and perhaps she too was getting a quick glimpse of a straining demon because she said, "You look tired, Charles. Go and rest till lunch."

"Go and rest where?" he said and he was still angry. "I am not going to stir out of here until something is done about that girl."

"Merricat? Why should anything be done? I said I would clean your room."

"Aren't you even going to punish her?"

"Punish me?" I was standing then, shivering against the door frame. "Punish me? You mean send me to bed without my dinner?"

And I ran. I ran until I was in the field of grass, in the very center where it was safe, and I sat there, the grass taller than my head and hiding me. Jonas found me, and we sat there together where no one could ever see us.

After a very long time I stood up again because I knew where I was going. I was going to the summerhouse. I had not been near the summerhouse for six years, but Charles had blackened the world and only the summerhouse would do. Jonas would not follow me; he disliked the summerhouse and when he saw me turning onto the overgrown path which led there he went another way as though he had something important to do and would meet me somewhere later. No one had ever liked the summerhouse very much, I remembered. Our father had planned it and had intended to lead the creek near it and build a tiny waterfall, but something had gotten into the wood and stone and paint when the summerhouse was built and made it bad. Our mother had once seen a rat in the doorway looking in and nothing after that could persuade her there again, and where our mother did not go, no one else went.

I had never buried anything around here. The ground was black and wet and nothing buried would have been quite comfortable. The trees pressed too closely against the sides of the summerhouse, and breathed heavily on its roof, and the poor flowers planted here once had either died or grown into huge tasteless wild things. When I stood near the summerhouse and looked at it I thought it the ugliest place I had ever seen; I remembered that our mother had quite seriously asked to have it burned down.

Inside was all wet and dark. I disliked sitting on the stone floor but there was no other place; once, I recalled, there had been chairs here and perhaps even a low table but these were gone now, carried off or rotted away. I sat on the floor and placed all of them correctly in my mind, in the circle around the dining-room table. Our father sat at the head. Our mother sat at the foot. Uncle Julian sat on one hand of our mother, and our brother Thomas on the other; beside my father sat our Aunt Dorothy and Constance. I sat between Constance and Uncle Julian, in my rightful, my own and proper, place at the table. Slowly I began to listen to them talking.

"—to buy a book for Mary Katherine. Lucy, should not Mary Katherine have a new book?"

"Mary Katherine should have anything she wants, my dear. Our most loved daughter must have anything she likes."

"Constance, your sister lacks butter. Pass it to her at once, please."

"Mary Katherine, we love you."

"You must never be punished. Lucy, you are to see to it that our most loved daughter Mary Katherine is never punished."

"Mary Katherine would never allow herself to do anything wrong; there is never any need to punish her."

"I have heard, Lucy, of disobedient children being sent to their beds without dinner as a punishment. That must not be permitted with our Mary Katherine."

"I quite agree, my dear. Mary Katherine must never be punished. Must never be sent to bed without her dinner. Mary

8

I had to go back for dinner; it was vital that I sit at the dinner table with Constance and Uncle Julian and Charles. It was unthinkable that they should sit there, eating their dinner and talking and passing food to one another, and see my place empty. As Jonas and I came along the path and through the garden in the gathering darkness I looked at the house with all the richness of love I contained; it was a good house, and soon it would be cleaned and fair again. I stopped for a minute, looking, and Jonas brushed my leg and spoke softly, in curiosity.

"I'm looking at our house," I told him and he stood quietly beside me, looking up with me. The roof pointed firmly against the sky, and the walls met one another compactly, and the windows shone darkly; it was a good house, and nearly clean. There was light from the kitchen window and from the windows of the dining room; it was time for their dinner and I must be there. I wanted to be inside the house, with the door shut behind me.

When I opened the kitchen door to go inside I could feel at once that the house still held anger, and I wondered that anyone could keep one emotion so long; I could hear his voice clearly from the kitchen, going on and on.

"—*must* be done about her," he was saying, "things simply can*not* continue like this."

Poor Constance, I thought, having to listen and listen and watch the food getting cold. Jonas ran ahead of me into the dining room, and Constance said, "Here she is."

I sood in the dining-room doorway and looked carefully for a minute. Constance was wearing pink, and her hair was combed back nicely; she smiled at me when I looked at her, and I knew she was tired of listening. Uncle Julian's wheel chair was pushed up tight against the table and I was sorry to see that Constance had tucked his napkin under his chin; it was too bad that Uncle Julian should not be allowed to eat freely. He was eating meat loaf, and peas which Constance had preserved one fragrant summer day; Constance had cut the meat loaf into small pieces and Uncle Julian mashed meat loaf and peas with the back of his spoon and stirred them before trying to get them into his mouth. He was not listening, but the voice went on and on.

"So you decided to come back again, did you? And high time, too, young lady; your sister and I have been trying to decide how to teach you a lesson."

"Wash your face, Merricat," Constance said gently. "And comb your hair; we do not want you untidy at table, and your Cousin Charles is already angry with you."

Charles pointed his fork at me. "I may as well tell you, Mary, that your tricks are over for good. Your sister and I have decided that we have had just exactly enough of hiding and destroying and temper."

I disliked having a fork pointed at me and I disliked the sound of the voice never stopping; I wished he would put food on the fork and put it into his mouth and strangle himself.

"Run along, Merricat," Constance said, "your dinner will be cold." She knew I would not eat dinner sitting at that table and she would bring me my dinner in the kitchen afterwards, but I thought that she did not want to remind Charles of that and so give him one more thing to talk about. I smiled at her and went into the hall, with the voice still talking behind me. There had not been this many words sounded in our house for a long time, and it was going to take a while to clean them out. I walked heavily going up the stairs so they could hear that I was surely going up, but when I reached the top I went as softly as Jonas behind me.

Constance had cleaned the room where he was living. It looked very empty, because all she had done was take things out; she had nothing to put back because I had carried all of it to the attic. I knew the dresser drawers were empty, and the closet, and the bookshelves. There was no mirror, and a broken watch and a smashed chain lay alone on the dresser top. Constance had taken away the wet bedding, and I supposed she had dried and turned the mattress, because the bed was made up again. The long curtains were gone, perhaps to be washed. He had been lying on the bed, because it was disarranged, and his pipe, still burning, lay on the table beside the bed; I supposed that he had been lying here when Constance called him to dinner, and I wondered if he had looked around and around the altered room, trying to find something familiar, hoping that perhaps the angle of the closet door or the light on the ceiling would bring everything back to him again. I was sorry that Constance had to turn the mattress alone; usually I helped her but perhaps he had come and offered to do it for her. She had even brought him a clean saucer for his pipe; our house did not have ashtrays and when he kept trying to find places to put down his pipe Constance had brought a set of chipped saucers from the pantry shelf and given them to him to hold his pipe. The saucers were pink, with gold leaves around the rim; they were from a set older than any I remembered.

"Who used them?" I asked Constance, when she brought them into the kitchen. "Where are their cups?"

"I've never seen them used; they come from a time before I was in the kitchen. Some great-grandmother brought them with her dowry and they were used and broken and replaced and finally put away on the top shelf of the pantry; there are only these saucers and three dinner plates."

"They belong in the pantry," I said. "Not put around the house."

Constance had given them to Charles and now they were scattered, instead of spending their little time decently put away on a shelf. There was one in the drawing room and one in the dining room and one, I supposed, in the study. They were not fragile, because the one now in the bedroom had not cracked although the pipe on it was burning. I had known all day that I would find something here; I brushed the saucer and the pipe off the table into the wastebasket and they fell softly onto the newspapers he had brought into the house.

I was wondering about my eyes; one of my eyes—the left—saw everything golden and yellow and orange, and the other eye saw shades of blue and grey and green; perhaps one eye was for daylight and the other was for night. If everyone in the world saw different colors from different eyes there might be a great many new colors still to be invented. I had reached the staircase to go downstairs before I remembered and had to go back to wash, and comb my hair. "What took you so long?" he asked when I sat down at the table. "What have you been doing up there?"

"Will you make me a cake with pink frosting?" I asked Constance. "With little gold leaves around the edge? Jonas and I are going to have a party."

"Perhaps tomorrow," Constance said.

"We are going to have a long talk after dinner," Charles said.

"*Solanum dulcamara,*" I told him.

"What?" he said.

"Deadly nightshade," Constance said. "Charles, please let it wait."

"I've had enough," he said.

"Constance?"

"Yes, Uncle Julian?"

"I have cleaned my plate." Uncle Julian found a morsel of meat loaf on his napkin and put it into his mouth. "What do I have now?"

"Perhaps a little more, Uncle Julian? It is a pleasure to see you so hungry."

"I feel considerably better tonight. I have not felt so hearty for days."

I was pleased that Uncle Julian was well and I knew he was happy because he had been so discourteous to Charles. While Constance was cutting up another small piece of meat loaf Uncle Julian looked at Charles with an evil shine in his old eyes, and I knew he was going to say something wicked. "Young man," he began at last, but Charles turned his head suddenly to look into the hall.

"I smell smoke," Charles said.

Constance paused and lifted her head and turned to the kitchen door. "The stove?" she said and got up quickly to go into the kitchen.

"Young man—"

"There is certainly smoke." Charles went to look into the hall. "I smell it out here," he said. I wondered whom he thought he was talking to; Constance was in the kitchen and Uncle Julian was thinking about what he was going to say, and I had stopped listening. "There *is* smoke," Charles said.

"It's not the stove." Constance stood in the kitchen doorway and looked at Charles.

Charles turned and came closer to me. "If this is anything you've done . . ." he said.

I laughed because it was clear that Charles was afraid to go upstairs and follow the smoke; then Constance said, "Charles—your pipe—" and he turned and ran up the stairs. "I've asked him and asked him," Constance said.

"Would it start a fire?" I asked her, and then Charles screamed from upstairs, screamed, I thought, with the exact sound of a bluejay in the woods. "That's Charles," I said politely to Constance, and she hurried to go into the hall and look up. "What *is* it?" she asked, "Charles, what *is* it?"

"Fire," Charles said, crashing down the stairs, "Run, run; the whole damn house is on fire," he screamed into Constance's face, "and you haven't got a *phone.*"

"My papers," Uncle Julian said. "I shall collect my papers and remove them to a place of safety." He pushed against the edge of the table to move his chair away. "Constance?"

"Run," Charles said, at the front door now, wrenching at the lock, "*run,* you fool."

"I have not done much running in the past few years, young man. I see no cause for this hysteria; there is time to gather my papers."

Charles had the front door open now, and turned on the doorsill to call to Constance. "Don't try to carry the safe," he said, "put the money in a bag. I'll be back as fast as I can get help. Don't panic." He ran, and we could hear him screaming "Fire! Fire! Fire!" as he ran toward the village.

"Good heavens," Constance said, almost amused. Then she took Uncle Julian's chair to help him into his room and I went into the hall and looked upstairs. Charles had left the door to our father's room standing open and I could see the movement of fire inside. Fire burns upward, I thought; it will burn their things in the attic. Charles had left the front door open too, and a line of smoke reached down the stairs and drifted outside. I did not see any need to move quickly or to run shrieking around the house because the fire did not seem to be hurrying itself. I wondered if I could go up the stairs and shut the door to our father's room and keep the fire inside, belonging entirely to Charles, but when I started up the stairs I saw a finger of flame reach out to touch the hall carpet and some heavy object fell crashing in our father's room. There would be nothing of Charles in there now; even his pipe must have been consumed.

"Uncle Julian is gathering his papers," Constance said, coming into the hall to stand beside me. She had Uncle Julian's shawl over her arm.

"We will have to go outside," I said. I knew that she was frightened, so I said, "We can stay on the porch, behind the vines, in the darkness."

"We neatened it just the other day," she said. "It has no *right* to burn." She began to shiver as though she were angry, and I took her by the hand and brought her through the open front door and just as we turned back for another look the lights came into the driveway with the disgusting noise of sirens and we were held in the doorway in the light. Constance put her face against me to hide, and then there was Jim Donell, the first one to leap from the fire engine and run up the steps. "Out of the way," he said, and pushed past us and into our house. I took Constance along the porch to the corner where the vines grew thick, and she moved into the corner and pressed against the vines. I held her hand tight, and together we watched the great feet of the men stepping across our doorsill, dragging their hoses, bringing filth and confusion and danger into our house. More lights moved into the driveway and up to the steps, and the front of the house was white and pale and uncomfortable at being so clearly visible; it had never been lighted before. The noise was too much for me to hear all together, but somewhere in the noise was Charles' voice, still going on and on. "Get the safe in the study," he said a thousand times.

Smoke squeezed out the front door, coming between the big men pushing in. "Constance," I whispered, "Constance, don't watch them."

"Can they see me?" she whispered back. "Is anyone looking?"

"They're all watching the fire. Be very quiet."

I looked carefully out between the vines. There was a long row of cars, and the village fire engine, all parked as close to the house as they could get, and everyone in the village was there, looking up and watching. I saw faces laughing, and faces that looked frightened, and then someone called out, very near to us, "What about the women, and the old man? Anyone see them?"

"They had plenty of warning," Charles shouted from somewhere, "they're all right."

Uncle Julian could manage his chair well enough to get out the back door, I thought, but it did not seem that the fire was going near the kitchen or Uncle Julian's room; I could see the hoses and hear the men shouting, and they were all on the stairs and in the front bedrooms upstairs. I could not get through the front door, and even if I could leave Constance there was no way to go around to the back door without going down the steps in the light with all of them watching. "Was Uncle Julian frightened?" I whispered to Constance.

"I think he was annoyed," she said. A few minutes later she said, "It will take a great deal of scrubbing to get that hall clean again," and sighed. I was pleased that she thought of the house and forgot the people outside.

"Jonas?" I said to her; "where is he?"

I could see her smile a little in the darkness of the vines. "He was annoyed, too," she said. "He went out the back door when I took Uncle Julian in to get his papers."

We were all right. Uncle Julian might very well forget that there was a fire at all if he became interested in his papers, and Jonas was almost certainly watching from the shadow of the trees. When they had finished putting out Charles' fire I would take Constance back inside and we could start to clean our house again. Constance was quieter, although more and more cars came down the driveway and the unending patter of feet went back and forth across our doorsill. Except for Jim Donell, who wore a hat proclaiming him "Chief," it was impossible to identify any one person, any more than it was possible to put a name to any of the faces out in front of our house, looking up and laughing at the fire.

I tried to think clearly. The house was burning; there was fire inside our house, but Jim Donell and the other, anonymous, men in hats and raincoats were curiously able to destroy the fire which was running through the bones of our house. It was Charles' fire. When I listened particularly for the fire I could hear it, a singing hot noise upstairs, but over and around it, smothering it, were the voices of the men inside and the voices of the people watching outside and the distant sound of cars on the driveway. Next to me Constance was standing quietly, sometimes looking at the men going into the house, but more often covering her eyes with her hands; she was excited, I thought, but not in any danger. Every now and then it was possible to hear one voice raised above the others; Jim Donell shouted some word of instruction, or someone in the crowd called out. "Why not let it burn?" a woman's voice came loudly, laughing, and "Get the safe out of the study downstairs"; that was Charles, safely in the crowd out front.

"Why not let it burn?" the woman called insistently, and one of the dark men going in and out of our front door turned and waved and grinned. "We're the firemen," he called back, "we *got* to put it out."

"Let it burn," the woman called.

Smoke was everywhere, thick and ugly. Sometimes when I looked out the faces of the people were clouded with smoke, and it came out the front door in frightening waves. Once there was a crash from inside the house and voices speaking quickly and urgently, and the faces outside turned up happily in the smoke, mouths open. "Get the safe," Charles called out wildly, "two or three of you men get the safe out of the study; the whole house is going."

"Let it burn," the woman called.

I was hungry and I wanted my dinner, and I wondered how long they could make the fire last before they put it out and went away and Constance and I could go back inside. One or two of the village boys had edged onto the porch dangerously close to where we stood, but they only looked inside, not at the porch, and tried to stand on their toes and see past the firemen and the hoses. I was tired and I wished it would all be over. I realized then that the light was lessening, the faces on the lawn less distinct, and a new tone came into the noise; the voices inside were surer, less sharp, almost pleased, and the voices outside were lower, and disappointed.

"It's going out," someone said.

"Under control," another voice added.

"Did a lot of damage, though." There was laughter. "Sure made a mess of the old place."

"Should of burned it down years ago."

"And them in it."

They mean us, I thought, Constance and me.

"Say—anybody *seen* them?"

"No such luck. Firemen threw them out."

"Too bad."

The light was almost gone. The people outside stood now in shadows, their faces narrowed and dark, with only the headlights of the cars to light them; I saw the flash of a smile, and somewhere else a hand raised to wave, and the voices went on regretfully.

"Just about over."

"Pretty good fire."

Jim Donell came through the front door. Everyone knew him because of his size and his hat saying CHIEF. "Say, Jim," someone called, "why don't you let it burn?"

He lifted both his hands to make everyone be quiet. "Fire's all out, folks," he said.

Very carefully he put up his hands and took off his hat saying CHIEF and while everyone watched he walked slowly down the steps and over to the fire engine and set his hat down on the front seat. Then he bent down, searching thoughtfully, and finally, while everyone watched, he took up a rock. In complete silence he turned slowly and then raised his arm and smashed the rock through one of the great tall windows of our mother's drawing room. A wall of laughter rose and grew behind him and then, first the boys on the steps and then the other men and at last the women and the smaller children, they moved like a wave at our house.

"Constance," I said, "Constance," but she had her hands over her eyes.

The other of the drawing-room windows crashed, this time from inside, and I saw that it had been shattered by the lamp which always stood by Constance's chair in the drawing room.

Above it all, most horrible, was the laughter. I saw one of the Dresden figurines thrown and break against the porch rail, and the other fell unbroken and rolled along the grass. I heard Constance's harp go over with a musical cry, and a sound which I knew was a chair being smashed against the wall.

"Listen," said Charles from somewhere, "will a couple of you guys help me with this safe?"

Then, through the laughter, someone began, "Merricat, said Constance, would you like a cup of tea?" It was rhythmic and insistent. I am on the moon, I thought, please let me be on the moon. Then I heard the sound of dishes smashing and at that minute realized that we stood outside the tall windows of the dining room and they were coming very close.

"Constance," I said, "we have to run."

She shook her head, her hands over her face.

"They'll find us in a minute. Please, Constance dearest; run with me."

"I can't," she said, and from just inside the dining-room window a shout went up: "Merricat, said Constance, would you like to go to sleep?" and I pulled Constance away a second before the window went; I thought a chair had been thrown through it, perhaps the dining-room chair where our father used to sit and Charles used to sit. "Hurry," I said, no longer able to be quiet in all that noise, and pulling Constance by the hand I ran toward the steps. As we came into the light she threw Uncle Julian's shawl across her face to hide it.

A little girl ran out of the front door carrying something, and her mother, behind her, caught her by the back of the dress and slapped her hands. "Don't you put that stuff in your mouth," the mother screamed, and the little girl dropped a handful of Constance's spice cookies.

"Merricat, said Constance, would you like a cup of tea?"

"Merricat, said Constance, would you like to go to sleep?"

"Oh, no, said Merricat, you'll poison me."

We had to get down the steps and into the woods to be safe; it was not far but the headlights of the cars shone across the lawn. I wondered if Constance would slip and fall, running through the light, but we had to get to the woods and there was no other way. We hesitated near the steps, neither one of us quite daring to go farther, but the windows were broken and inside they were throwing our dishes and our glasses and our silverware and even the pots Constance used in cooking; I wondered if my stool in the corner of the kitchen had been smashed yet. While we stood still for a last minute, a car came up the driveway, and another behind it; they swung to a stop in front of the house, sending more light onto the lawn. "What the holy devil is going *on* here?" Jim Clarke said, rolling out of the first car, and Helen Clarke, on the other side, opened her mouth and stared. Shouting and pushing, and not seeing us at all, Jim Clarke made his way through our door and into our house, "What the holy goddam devil is going *on* here?" he kept saying and outside Helen Clarke never saw us, but only stared at our house. "Crazy fools," Jim Clarke yelled inside, "crazy drunken fools." Dr. Levy came out of the second car and hurried toward the house. "Has everyone gone crazy in here?" Jim Clarke was saying from inside, and there was a shout of laughter. "Would you like a cup of tea?" someone inside screamed, and they laughed. "Ought to bring it down brick by brick," someone said inside.

The doctor came up the steps running, and pushed us aside without looking. "Where is Julian Blackwood?" he asked a woman in the doorway, and the woman said, "Down in the boneyard ten feet deep."

It was time; I took Constance tightly by the hand, and we started carefully down the steps. I would not run yet because I was afraid that Constance might fall, so I brought her slowly down the steps; no one could see us yet except Helen Clarke and she stared at the house. Behind us I heard Jim Clarke shouting; he was trying to make the people leave our house, and before we reached the bottom step there were voices behind us.

"There they are," someone shouted and I think it was Stella. "There they are, there they are, there they are," and I started to run but Constance stumbled and then they were all around us, pushing and laughing and trying to get close to see. Constance held Uncle Julian's shawl across her face so they could not look at her, and for a minute we stood very still, pressed together by the feeling of people all around us.

"Put them back in the house and start the fire all over again."

"We fixed things up nice for you girls, just like you always wanted it."

"Merricat, said Constance, would you like a cup of tea?"

For one terrible minute I thought that they were going to join hands and dance around us, singing. I saw Helen Clarke far away, pressed hard against the side of her car; she was crying and saying something and even though I could not hear her through the noise I knew she was saying "I want to go home, please, I want to go home."

"Merricat, said Constance, would you like to go to sleep?"

They were trying not to touch us; whenever I turned they fell back a little; once, between two shoulders I saw Harler of the junk yard wandering across the porch of our house, picking up things and setting them to one side in a pile. I moved a little, holding Constance's hand tight, and as they fell back we ran suddenly, going toward the trees, but Jim Donell's wife and Mrs. Mueller came in front of us, laughing and holding out their arms, and we stopped. I turned, and gave Constance a little pull, and we ran, but Stella and the Harris boys crossed in front of us, laughing, and the Harris boys shouting "Down in the boneyard ten feet deep," and we stopped. Then I turned toward the house, running again with Constance pulled behind me, and Elbert the grocer and his greedy wife were there, holding their hands to halt us, almost dancing together, and we stopped. I went then to the side, and Jim Donell stepped in front of us, and we stopped.

"Oh, no, said Merricat, you'll poison me," Jim Donell said politely, and they came around us again, circling and keeping carefully out of reach. "Merricat, said Constance, would you like to go to sleep?" Over it all was the laughter, almost drowning the singing and the shouting and the howling of the Harris boys.

"Merricat, said Constance, would you like a cup of tea?"

Constance held to me with one hand and with the other hand she kept Uncle Julian's shawl across her face. I saw an opening in the circle around us, and ran again for the trees, but all the Harris boys were there, one on the ground with laughter, and we stopped. I turned again and ran for the house but Stella came forward and we stopped. Constance was stumbling, and I wondered if we were going to fall onto the ground in front of them, lying there where they might step on us in their dancing, and I stood still; I could not possibly let Constance fall in front of them.

"That's all now," Jim Clarke said from the porch. His voice was not loud, but they all heard. "That's enough," he said. There was a small polite silence, and then someone said, "Down in the boneyard ten feet deep," and the laughter rose.

"Listen to me," Jim Clarke said, raising his voice, "listen to me. Julian Blackwood is dead."

Then they were quiet at last. After a minute Charles Blackwood said from the crowd around us, "Did she kill him?" They went back from us, moving slowly in small steps, withdrawing, until there was a wide clear space around us and Constance standing clearly with Uncle Julian's shawl across her face. "Did she kill him?" Charles Blackwood asked again.

"She did not," said the doctor, standing in the doorway of our house. "Julian died as I have always known he would; he has been waiting a long time."

"Now go quietly," Jim Clarke said. He began to take people by the shoulders, pushing a little at their backs, turning them toward their cars and the driveway. "Go quickly," he said, "There has been a death in this house."

It was so quiet, in spite of many people moving across the grass and going away, that I heard Helen Clarke say, "Poor Julian."

I took a cautious step toward the darkness, pulling Constance a little so that she followed me. "Heart," the doctor said on the porch, and I went another step. No one turned to look at us. Car doors slammed softly and motors started. I looked back once. A little group was standing around the doctor on the steps. Most of the lights were turned away, heading down the driveway. When I felt the shadows of the trees fall on us, I moved quickly; one last step and we were inside. Pulling Constance, I hurried under the trees, in the darkness; when I felt my feet leave the grass of the lawn and touch the soft mossy ground of the path through the woods and knew that the trees had closed in around us I stopped and put my arms around Constance. "It's all over," I told her, and held her tight. "It's all right," I said, "all right now."

I knew my way in the darkness or in the light. I thought once how good it was that I had straightened my hiding place and freshened it, so it would now be pleasant for Constance. I would cover her with leaves, like children in a story, and keep her safe and warm. Perhaps I would sing to her or tell her stories; I would bring her bright fruits and berries and water in a leaf cup. Someday we would go to the moon. I found the entrance to my hiding place and led Constance in and took her to the corner where there was a fresh pile of leaves and a blanket. I pushed her gently until she sat down and I took Uncle Julian's shawl away from her and covered her with it. A little purr came from the corner and I knew that Jonas had been waiting here for me.

I put branches across the entrance; even if they came with lights they would not see us. It was not entirely dark; I could see the shadow that was Constance and when I put my head back I saw two or three stars, shining from far away between the leaves and the branches and down onto my head.

One of our mother's Dresden figurines is broken, I thought, and I said aloud to Constance, "I am going to put death in all their food and watch them die."

Constance stirred, and the leaves rustled. "The way you did before?" she asked.

It had never been spoken of between us, not once in six years.

"Yes," I said after a minute, "the way I did before."

9

Sometime during the night an ambulance came and took Uncle Julian away, and I wondered if they missed his shawl, which was wound around Constance as she slept. I saw the ambulance lights turning into the driveway, with the small red light on top, and I heard the distant sounds of Uncle Julian's leaving, the voices speaking gently because they were in the presence of the dead, and the doors opening and closing. They called to us two or three times, perhaps to ask if they might have Uncle Julian, but their voices were subdued and no one came into the woods. I sat by the creek, wishing that I had been kinder to Uncle Julian. Uncle Julian had believed that I was dead, and now he was dead himself; bow your heads to our beloved Mary Katherine, I thought, or you will be dead.

The water moved sleepily in the darkness and I wondered what kind of a house we would have now. Perhaps the fire had destroyed everything and we would go back tomorrow and find that the past six years had been burned and they were waiting for us, sitting around the dining-room table waiting for Constance to bring them their dinner. Perhaps we would find ourselves in the Rochester house, or living in the village or on a houseboat on the river or in a tower on top of a hill; perhaps the fire might be persuaded to reverse itself and abandon our house and destroy the village instead; perhaps the villagers were all dead now. Perhaps the village was really a great game board, with the squares neatly marked out, and I had been moved past the square which read "Fire; return to Start," and was now on the last few squares, with only one move to go to reach home.

Jonas's fur smelled of smoke. Today was Helen Clarke's day to come to tea, but there would be no tea today, because we would have to neaten the house, although it was not the usual day for neatening the house. I wished that Constance had made sandwiches for us to bring down to the creek, and I wondered if Helen Clarke would try to come to tea even though the house was not ready. I decided that from now on I would not be allowed to hand tea cups.

When it first began to get light I heard Constance stirring on the leaves and I went into my hiding place to be near her when she awakened. When she opened her eyes she looked first at the trees above her, and then at me and smiled.

"We are on the moon at last," I told her, and she smiled.

"I thought I dreamed it all," she said.

"It really happened," I said.

"Poor Uncle Julian."

"They came in the night and took him away, and we stayed here on the moon."

"I'm glad to be here," she said. "Thank you for bringing me."

There were leaves in her hair and dirt on her face and Jonas, who had followed me into my hiding place, stared at her in surprise; he had never seen Constance with a dirty face before. For a minute she was quiet, no longer smiling, looking back at Jonas, realizing that she was dirty, and then she said, "Merricat, what are we going to do?"

"First we must neaten the house, even though it is not the usual day."

"The house," she said. "Oh, Merricat."

"I had no dinner last night," I told her.

"Oh, *Merricat*." She sat up and untangled herself quickly from Uncle Julian's shawl and the leaves; "Oh, Merricat, poor baby," she said. "We'll hurry," and she scrambled to her feet.

"First you had better wash your face."

She went to the creek and wet her handkerchief and scrubbed at her face while I shook out Uncle Julian's shawl and folded it, thinking how strange and backward everything was this morning; I had never touched Uncle Julian's shawl before. I already saw that the rules were going to be different, but it was odd to be folding Uncle Julian's shawl. Later, I thought, I would come back here to my hiding place and clean it, and put in fresh leaves.

"Merricat, you'll starve."

"We have to watch," I said, taking her hand to slow her. "We have to go very quietly and carefully; some of them may still be around waiting."

I went first down the path, walking silently, with Constance and Jonas behind me. Constance could not step as silently as I could, but she made very little sound and of course Jonas made no sound at all. I took the path that would bring us out of the woods at the back of the house, near the vegetable garden, and when I came to the edge of the woods I stopped and held Constance back while we looked carefully to see if there were any of them left. For one first minute we saw only the garden and the kitchen door, looking just as always, and then Constance gasped and said, "Oh, *Merricat*," with a little moan, and I held myself very still, because the top of our house was gone.

I remembered that I had stood looking at our house with love yesterday, and I thought how it had always been so tall, reaching up into the trees. Today the house ended above the kitchen doorway in a nightmare of black and twisted wood; I saw part of a window frame still holding broken glass and I thought: that was my window; I looked out that window from my room.

There was no one there, and no sound. We moved together very slowly toward the house, trying to understand its ugliness and ruin and shame. I saw that ash had drifted among the vegetable plants; the lettuce would have to be washed before I could eat it, and the tomatoes. No fire had come this way, but everything, the grass and the apple trees and the marble bench in Constance's garden, had an air of smokiness and everything was dirty. As we came closer to the house we saw more clearly that the fire had not reached the ground floor, but had had to be content with the bedrooms and the attic. Constance hesitated at the kitchen door, but she had opened it a thousand times before and it ought surely to recognize the touch of her hand, so she took the latch and lifted it. The house seemed to shiver when she opened the door, although one more draft could hardly chill it now. Constance had to push at the door to make it open, but no burned timber crashed down, and there was not, as I half thought there might be, a sudden rushing falling together, as a house, seemingly solid but really made only of ash, might dissolve at a touch.

"My kitchen," Constance said. "My kitchen."

She stood in the doorway, looking. I thought that we had somehow not found our way back correctly through the night, that we had somehow lost ourselves and come back through the wrong gap in time, or the wrong door, or the wrong fairy tale. Constance put her hand against the door frame to steady herself, and said again, "My kitchen, Merricat."

"My stool is still there," I said.

The obstacle which made the door hard to open was the kitchen table, turned on its side. I set it upright, and we went inside. Two of the chairs had been smashed, and the floor was horrible with broken dishes and glasses and broken boxes of food and paper torn from the shelves. Jars of jam and syrup and catsup had been shattered against the walls. The sink where Constance washed her dishes was filled with broken glass, as though glass after glass had been broken there methodically, one after another. Drawers of silverware and cooking ware had been pulled out and broken against the table and the walls, and silverware that had been in the house for generations of Blackwood wives was lying bent and scattered on the floor. Tablecloths and napkins hemmed by Blackwood women, and washed and ironed again and again, mended and cherished, had been ripped from the dining-room sideboard and dragged across the kitchen. It seemed that all the wealth and hidden treasure of our house had been found out and torn and soiled; I saw broken plates which had come from the top shelves in the cupboard, and our little sugar bowl with roses lay almost at my feet, handles gone. Constance bent down and picked up a silver spoon. "This was our grandmother's wedding pattern," she said, and set the spoon on the table. Then she said, "The preserves," and turned to the cellar door; it was closed and I hoped that perhaps they had not seen it, or had perhaps not had time to go down the stairs. Constance picked her way carefully across the floor and opened the cellar door and looked down. I thought of the jars and jars so beautifully preserved lying in broken sticky heaps in the cellar, but Constance went down a step or two and said, "No, it's all right; nothing here's been touched." She closed the cellar door again and made her way across to the sink to wash her hands and dry them on a dishtowel from the floor. "First, your breakfast," she said.

Jonas sat on the doorstep in the growing sunlight looking at the kitchen with astonishment; once he raised his eyes to me and I wondered if he thought that Constance and I had made this mess. I saw a cup not broken, and picked it up and set it on the table, and then thought to look for more things which might have escaped. I remembered that one of our mother's Dresden figurines had rolled safely onto the grass and I wondered if it had hidden successfully and preserved itself; I would look for it later.

Nothing was orderly, nothing was planned; it was not like any other day. Once Constance went into the cellar and came back with her arms full. "Vegetable soup," she said, almost singing, "and strawberry jam, and chicken soup, and pickled beef." She set the jars on the kitchen table and turned slowly, looking down at the floor. "There," she said at last, and went to a corner to pick up a small saucepan. Then on a sudden thought she set down the saucepan and made her way into the pantry. "Merricat," she called with laughter, "they didn't find the flour in the barrel. Or the salt. Or the potatoes."

They found the sugar, I thought. The floor was gritty, and almost alive under my feet, and I thought of course; of course they would go looking for the sugar and have a lovely time; perhaps they had thrown handfuls of sugar at one another, screaming, "Blackwood sugar, Blackwood sugar, want a taste?"

"They got to the pantry shelves," Constance went on, "the cereals and the spices and the canned food."

I walked slowly around the kitchen, looking at the floor. I thought that they had probably tumbled things by the armload, because cans of food were scattered and bent as though they had been tossed into the air, and the boxes of cereal and tea and crackers had been trampled under foot and broken open. The

tins of spices were all together, thrown into a corner unopened;
I thought I could still smell the faint spicy scent of Constance's
cookies and then saw some of them, crushed on the floor.

Constance came out of the pantry carrying a loaf of bread.
"Look what they didn't find," she said, "and there are eggs and
milk and butter in the cooler." Since they had not found the cellar door they had not found the cooler just inside, and I was
pleased that they had not discovered eggs to mix into the mess
on the floor.

At one time I found three unbroken chairs and set them
where they belonged around the table. Jonas sat in my corner,
on my stool, watching us. I drank chicken soup from a cup
without a handle, and Constance washed a knife to spread butter on the bread. Although I did not perceive it then, time and
the orderly pattern of our old days had ended; I do not know
when I found the three chairs and when I ate buttered bread,
whether I had found the chairs and then eaten bread, or whether
I had eaten first, or even done both at once. Once Constance
turned suddenly and put down her knife; she started for the
closed door to Uncle Julian's room and then turned back, smiling a little. "I thought I heard him waking," she said, and sat
down again.

We had not yet been out of the kitchen. We still did not know
how much house was left to us, or what we might find waiting
beyond the closed doors into the dining room and the hall. We
sat quietly in the kitchen, grateful for the chairs and the chicken
soup and the sunlight coming through the doorway, not yet
ready to go further.

"What will they do with Uncle Julian?" I asked.

"They will have a funeral," Constance said with sadness.
"Do you remember the others?"

"I was in the orphanage."

"They let me go to the funerals of the others. I can remember.
They will have a funeral for Uncle Julian, and the Clarkes will
go, and the Carringtons, and certainly little Mrs. Wright. They
will tell each other how sorry they are. They will look to see if
we are there."

I felt them looking to see if we were there, and I shivered.

"They will bury him with the others."

"I would like to bury something for Uncle Julian," I said.

Constance was quiet, looking at her fingers which lay still and long on the table. "Uncle Julian is gone, and the others," she said. "Most of our house is gone, Merricat; we are all that is left."

"Jonas."

"Jonas. We are going to lock ourselves in more securely than ever."

"But today is the day Helen Clarke comes to tea."

"No," she said. "Not again. Not here."

As long as we sat quietly together in the kitchen it was possible to postpone seeing the rest of the house. The library books were still on their shelf, untouched, and I supposed that no one had wanted to touch books belonging to the library; there was a fine, after all, for destroying library property.

Constance, who was always dancing, seemed now unwilling to move; she sat on at the kitchen table with her hands spread before her, not looking around at the destruction, and almost dreaming, as though she never believed that she had wakened this morning at all. "We must neaten the house," I said to her uneasily, and she smiled across at me.

When I felt that I could not wait for her any longer I said, "I'm going to look," and got up and went to the dining-room door. She watched me, not moving. When I opened the door to the dining room there was a shocking smell of wetness and burned wood and destruction, and glass from the tall windows lay across the floor and the silver tea service had been swept off the sideboard and stamped into grotesque, unrecognizable shapes. Chairs were broken here, too; I remembered that they had taken up chairs and hurled them at windows and walls. I went through the dining room and into the front hall. The front door stood wide open and early sunlight lay in patterns along the floor of the hall, touching broken glass and torn cloth; after a minute I recognized the cloth as the drawing-room draperies which our mother had once had made up fourteen feet long. No one was outside; I stood in the open doorway and saw that the lawn was marked with the tires of

cars and the feet which had danced, and where the hoses had
gone there were puddles and mud. The front porch was littered, and I remembered the neat pile of partly broken furniture which Harler the junk dealer had set together last night. I
wondered if he planned to come today with a truck and gather
up everything he could, or if he had only put the pile together
because he loved great piles of broken things and could not resist stacking junk wherever he found it. I waited in the doorway to be sure that no one was watching, and then I ran down
the steps across the grass and found our mother's Dresden figurine unbroken where it had hidden against the roots of a
bush; I thought to take it to Constance.

She was still sitting quietly at the kitchen table, and when I
put the Dresden figurine down before her she looked for a
minute and then took it in her hands and held it against her
cheek. "It was all my fault," she said. "Somehow it was all my
fault."

"I love you, Constance," I said.

"And I love you, Merricat."

"And will you make that little cake for Jonas and me? Pink
frosting, with gold leaves around the edge?"

She shook her head, and for a minute I thought she was not
going to answer me, and then she took a deep breath, and stood
up. "First," she said, "I'm going to clean this kitchen."

"What are you going to do with that?" I asked her, touching
the Dresden figurine with the very tip of my finger.

"Put it back where it belongs," she said, and I followed her
as she opened the door to the hall and made her way down the
hall to the drawing-room doorway. The hall was less littered
than the rooms, because there had been less in it to smash, but
there were fragments carried from the kitchen, and we stepped
on spoons and dishes which had been thrown here. I was
shocked when we came into the drawing room to see our
mother's portrait looking down on us graciously while her
drawing room lay destroyed around her. The white wedding-
cake trim was blackened with smoke and soot and would never
be clean again; I disliked seeing the drawing room even more
than the kitchen or the dining room, because we had always

kept it so tidy, and our mother had loved this room. I wondered which of them had pushed over Constance's harp and I remembered that I had heard it cry out as it fell. The rose brocade on the chairs was torn and dirty, smudged with the marks of wet feet that had kicked at the chairs and stamped on the sofa. The windows were broken here too, and with the drapes torn down we were clearly visible from outside.

"I think I can close the shutters," I said, as Constance hesitated in the doorway, unwilling to come further into the room. I stepped out onto the porch through the broken window, thinking that no one had ever come this way before, and found that I could unhook the shutters easily. The shutters were as tall as the windows; originally it was intended that a man with a ladder would close the shutters when the summers were ended and the family went away to a city house, but so many years had passed since the shutters were closed that the hooks had rusted and I needed only to shake the heavy shutters to pull the hooks away from the house. I swung the shutters closed, but I could only reach the lower bolt to hold them; there were two more bolts high above my head; perhaps some night I might come out here with a ladder, but the lower bolt would have to hold them now. After I had closed the shutters on both tall drawing-room windows I went along the porch and in, formally, through the front door and into the drawing room where Constance stood in dimness now, without the sunlight. Constance went to the mantel and set the Dresden figurine in its place below the portrait of our mother and for one quick minute the great shadowy room came back together again, as it should be, and then fell apart forever.

We had to walk carefully because of the broken things on the floor. Our father's safe lay just inside the drawing-room door, and I laughed and even Constance smiled, because it had not been opened and it had clearly not been possible to carry it any farther than this. "Foolishness," Constance said, and touched the safe with her toe.

Our mother had always been pleased when people admired her drawing room, but now no one could come to the windows and look in, and no one would ever see it again. Constance and

I closed the drawing-room door behind us and never opened it afterwards. Constance waited just inside the front door while I went onto the porch again and closed the shutters over the tall dining-room windows, and then I came inside and we shut and locked the front door and we were safe. The hall was dark, with two narrow lines of sunlight coming through the two narrow glass panels set on either side of the door; we could look outside through the glass, but no one could see in, even by putting their eyes up close, because the hall inside was dark. Above us the stairs were black and led into blackness or burned rooms with, incredibly, tiny spots of sky showing through. Until now, the roof had always hidden us from the sky, but I did not think that there was any way we could be vulnerable from above, and closed my mind against the thought of silent winged creatures coming out of the trees above to perch on the broken burnt rafters of our house, peering down. I thought it might be wise to barricade the stairs by putting something—a broken chair, perhaps—across. A mattress, soaked and dirty, lay halfway down the stairs; this was where they had stood with the hoses and fought the fire back and out. I stood at the foot of the stairs, looking up, wondering where our house had gone, the walls and the floors and the beds and the boxes of things in the attic; our father's watch was burned away, and our mother's tortoise-shell dressing set. I could feel a breath of air on my cheek; it came from the sky I could see, but it smelled of smoke and ruin. Our house was a castle, turreted and open to the sky.

"Come back to the kitchen," Constance said. "I can't stay out here."

Like children hunting for shells, or two old ladies going through dead leaves looking for pennies, we shuffled along the kitchen floor with our feet, turning over broken trash to find things which were still whole, and useful. When we had been along and across and diagonally through the kitchen we had gathered together a little pile of practical things on the kitchen table, and there was quite enough for the two of us. There were two cups with handles, and several without, and half a dozen plates, and three bowls. We had been able to rescue all the cans of food undamaged, and the cans of spice went neatly back onto their shelf. We found most of the silverware and straightened most of it as well as we could and put it back into its proper drawers. Since every Blackwood bride had brought her own silverware and china and linen into the house we had always had dozens of butter knives and soup ladles and cake servers; our mother's best silverware had been in a tarnish-proof box in the dining-room sideboard, but they had found it and scattered it on the floor.

One of our whole cups was green with a pale yellow inside, and Constance said that one could be mine. "I never saw anyone use it before," she said. "I suppose a grandmother or a great-great-aunt brought that set to the house as her wedding china. There once were plates to match." The cup which Constance chose was white with orange flowers, and one of the plates matched that. "I remember when we used those dishes," Constance said; "they were the everyday china when I was very small. The china we used for best then was white, with gold edges. Then Mother bought new best china and the white and gold china was used for everyday and these flowered dishes went onto the pantry shelf with the other half-broken sets. These last few years I have always used Mother's everyday china, except when Helen Clarke came to tea. We will take our meals like ladies," she said, "using cups with handles."

When we had taken out everything we wanted and could use, Constance got the heavy broom and swept all the rubble into the dining room. "Now we won't have to look at it," she said. She swept the hall clear so we could go from the kitchen to the front door without passing through the dining room, and then we closed all the doors to the dining room and never opened them again. I thought of the Dresden figurine standing small and courageous under our mother's portrait in the dark drawing room and I remembered that we would never dust it again. Before Constance swept away the torn cloth that had been the drawing-room drapes I asked her to cut me off a piece of the cord which had once drawn them open and shut, and she cut me a piece with a gold tassel on the end; I wondered if it might be the right thing to bury for Uncle Julian.

When we had finished and Constance had scrubbed the kitchen floor our house looked clean and new; from the front door to the kitchen door everything was clear and swept. So many things were gone from the kitchen that it looked bare, but Constance put our cups and plates and bowls on a shelf, and found a pan to give Jonas milk, and we were quite safe. The front door was locked, and the kitchen door was locked and bolted, and we were sitting at the kitchen table drinking milk from our two cups and Jonas was drinking from his pan when a knocking started on the front door. Constance ran to the cellar, and I stopped just long enough to be sure that the kitchen door was bolted, and then followed her. We sat on the cellar stairs in the darkness, and listened. Far away, at the front door, the knocking went on and on, and then a voice called, "Constance? Mary Katherine?"

"It's Helen Clarke," Constance said in a whisper.

"Do you think she has come for her tea?"

"No. Never again."

As we had both known she would, she came around the house, calling us. When she knocked on the kitchen door we held our breath, neither of us moving, because the top half of the kitchen door was glass, and we knew she could see in, but we were safely on the cellar stairs and she could not open the door.

"Constance? Mary Katherine? Are you *in* there?" She shook the door handle as people do when they want a door to open and think to catch it unaware and slip in before the lock can hold. "Jim," she said, "I *know* they're in there. I can see something cooking on the stove. You've got to open the door," she said, raising her voice. "Constance, come and talk to me; I want to see you. Jim," she said, "they're in there and they can hear me, I know it."

"I'm sure they can hear you," Jim Clarke said. "They can probably hear you in the village."

"But I'm sure they misunderstood the people last night; I'm sure Constance was upset, and I *must* tell them that nobody meant any harm. Constance, listen to me, please. We want you and Mary Katherine to come to our house until we can decide what to do with you. Everything's all right, really it is; we're going to forget all about it."

"Do you think she will push over the house?" I whispered to Constance, and Constance shook her head wordlessly.

"Jim, do you think you could break down the door?"

"Certainly not. Leave them alone, Helen, they'll come out when they're ready."

"But Constance takes these things so *seriously*. I'm sure she's frightened now."

"Leave them alone."

"They cannot be left alone, that is absolutely the worst possible thing for them. I want them out of there and home with me where I can take care of them."

"They don't seem to want to come," Jim Clarke said.

"Constance? Constance? I know you're in there; come and open the door."

I was thinking that we might very well put a cloth or a piece of cardboard over the window in the kitchen door; it simply would not do to have Helen Clarke constantly peering in to watch pots cooking on the stove. We could pin the curtains together across the kitchen windows, and perhaps if the windows were all covered we could sit quietly at the table when Helen Clarke came pounding outside and not have to hide on the cellar stairs.

"Let's leave," Jim Clarke said. "They're not going to answer you."

"But I want to take them home with me."

"We did what we could. We'll come back another time, when they'll feel more like seeing you."

"Constance? Constance, *please* answer me."

Constance sighed, and tapped her fingers irritably and almost noiselessly on the stair rail. "I wish she'd hurry," she said into my ear, "my soup is going to boil over."

Helen Clarke called again and again, going back around the house to their car, calling "Constance? Constance?" as though we might be somewhere in the woods, up a tree perhaps, or under the lettuce leaves, or waiting to spring out at her from behind a bush. When we heard their car start, distantly, we came up out of the cellar and Constance turned off her soup and I

went along the hall to the front door to be sure they had gone
and that the door was safely locked. I saw their car turn out of
the driveway and thought I could still hear Helen Clarke calling
"Constance? Constance?"

"She certainly wanted her tea," I said to Constance when I
came back to the kitchen.

"We have only two cups with handles," Constance said.
"She will never take tea here again."

"It's a good thing Uncle Julian's gone, or one of us would
have to use a broken cup. Are you going to neaten Uncle Julian's room?"

"Merricat." Constance turned from the stove to look at me.
"What are we going to do?"

"We've neatened the house. We've had food. We've hidden
from Helen Clarke. What *are* we going to do?"

"Where are we going to sleep? How are we going to know
what time it is? What will we wear for clothes?"

"Why do we need to know what time it is?"

"Our food won't last forever, even the preserves."

"We can sleep in my hiding place by the creek."

"No. That's all right for hiding, but you must have a real bed."

"I saw a mattress on the stairs. From my own old bed, perhaps. We can pull it down and clean it and dry it in the sun. One
corner is burned."

"Good," said Constance. We went together to the stairs and
took hold of the mattress awkwardly; it was unpleasantly wet
and dirty. We dragged it, pulling together, along the hall, with
little scraps of wood and glass coming with it, and got it across
Constance's clean kitchen floor to the kitchen door. Before un-
locking the door I looked out carefully, and even when the door
was opened I went out first to look around in every direction,
but it was safe. We dragged the mattress out onto the lawn, and
put it in the sun near our mother's marble bench.

"Uncle Julian used to sit right here," I said.

"It would be a good day, today, for Uncle Julian to sit in
the sun."

"I hope he was warm when he died. Perhaps he remembered
the sun for a minute."

"I had his shawl; I hope he didn't wish for it. Merricat, I am going to plant something here, where he used to sit."

"I am going to bury something for him. What will you plant?"

"A flower." Constance leaned, and touched the grass softly. "Some kind of a yellow flower."

"It's going to look funny, right in the middle of the lawn."

"We'll know why it's there, and no one else will ever see it."

"And I will bury something yellow, to keep Uncle Julian warm."

"First, however, my lazy Merricat, you will get a pot of water and scrub that mattress clean. And I will wash the kitchen floor again."

We were going to be very happy, I thought. There were a great many things to do, and a whole new pattern of days to arrange, but I thought we were going to be very happy. Constance was pale, and still saddened by what they had done to her kitchen, but she had scrubbed every shelf, and washed the table again and again, and washed the windows and the floor. Our dishes were bravely on their shelf, and the cans and unbroken boxes of food we had rescued made a substantial row in the pantry.

"I could train Jonas to bring back rabbits for stew," I told her, and she laughed, and Jonas looked back at her blandly.

"That cat is so used to living on cream and rum cakes and buttered eggs that I doubt if he could catch a grasshopper," she said.

"I don't think I could care for a grasshopper stew."

"At any rate, right *now* I am making an onion pie."

While Constance washed the kitchen I found a heavy cardboard carton which I took apart carefully, and so had several large pieces of cardboard to cover the glass window in the kitchen door. The hammer and the nails were in the tool shed where Charles Blackwood had put them after trying to mend the broken step, and I nailed cardboard across the kitchen door until the glass was completely covered and no one could see in. I nailed more cardboard across the two kitchen windows, and the kitchen was dark, but safe. "It would be safer to let the kitchen windows get dirty," I told Constance, but she was shocked, and said, "I wouldn't live in a house with dirty windows."

When we had finished the kitchen was very clean but could not sparkle because there was so little light, and I knew that Constance was not pleased. She loved sunshine and brightness and cooking in a light lovely kitchen. "We can keep the door open," I said, "if we watch carefully all the time. We'll hear if any cars stop in front of the house. When I can," I said, "I will try to think of a way to build barricades along the sides of the house so no one will be able to come around here to the back."

"I am sure Helen Clarke will try again."

"At any rate she cannot look in now."

The afternoon was drawing in; even with the door open the sunlight came only a short way across the floor, and Jonas came to Constance at the stove, asking for his supper. The kitchen was warm and comfortable and familiar and clean. It would be nice to have a fireplace in here, I thought; we could sit beside a fire, and then I thought no, we have already had a fire.

"I will go and make sure that the front door is locked," I said.

The front door was locked and no one was outside. When I came back into the kitchen Constance said, "Tomorrow I will clean Uncle Julian's room. We have so little house left that it should all be very clean."

"Will you sleep in there? In Uncle Julian's bed?"

"No, Merricat. I want you to sleep in there. It's the only bed we have."

"I am not allowed in Uncle Julian's room."

She was quiet for a minute, looking at me curiously, and then asked, "Even though Uncle Julian's gone, Merricat?"

"Besides, I found the mattress, and cleaned it, and it came from my bed. I want it on the floor in my corner."

"Silly Merricat. Anyway, I'm afraid we'll both have the floor tonight. The mattress will not dry before tomorrow, and Uncle Julian's bed is not clean."

"I can bring branches from my hiding place, and leaves."

"On my clean kitchen floor?"

"I'll get the blanket, though, and Uncle Julian's shawl."

"You're going out? Now? All that way?"

"No one's outside," I said. "It's almost dark and I can go very safely. If anyone comes, close the door and lock it; if I see that the door is closed I will wait by the creek until I can come safely home. And I will take Jonas for protection."

I ran all the way to the creek, but Jonas was faster, and was waiting for me when I got to my hiding place. It was good to run, and good to come back again to our house and see the kitchen door standing open and the warm light inside. When Jonas and I came in I shut the door and bolted it and we were ready for the night.

"It's a good dinner," Constance said, warm and happy from cooking. "Come and sit down, Merricat." With the door shut she had had to turn on the ceiling light, and our dishes on the table were neatly set. "Tomorrow I will try to polish the silverware," she said, "and we must bring in things from the garden."

"The lettuce is full of ashes."

"Tomorrow, too," Constance said, looking at the black squares of cardboard which covered the windows, "I am going to try to think of some kind of curtains to hide your cardboard."

"Tomorrow I will barricade the sides of the house. Tomorrow Jonas will catch us a rabbit. Tomorrow I will guess for you what time it is."

Far away, in the front of the house, a car stopped, and we were silent, looking at one another; now, I thought, now we will know how safe we are, and I got up and made sure that the kitchen door was bolted; I could not see out through the cardboard and I was sure that they could not see in. The knocking started at the front door, but there was no time to make sure that the front door was locked. They knocked only for a moment, as though certain that we would not be in the front of the house, and then we heard them stumbling in the darkness as they tried to find their way around the side of the house to the back. I heard Jim Clarke's voice, and another which I remembered was the voice of Dr. Levy.

"Can't see a thing," Jim Clarke said. "Black as sin out here."

"There's a crack of light at one of the windows."

Which one, I wondered; which window still showed a crack?

"They're in there, all right," Jim Clarke said. "No place else they could be."

"I just want to know if they're hurt, or sick; don't like to think of them shut up in there needing help."

"I'm supposed to bring them home with me," Jim Clarke said.

They came to the back door; their voices were directly outside, and Constance reached out her hand across the table to me; if it seemed that they might be able to look in we could run together for the cellar. "Damn place is all boarded up," Jim Clarke said, and I thought, good, oh, that's good. I had forgotten that there would be real boards in the tool shed; I never thought of anything but cardboard which is much too weak.

"Miss Blackwood?" the doctor called, and one of them knocked on the door. "Miss Blackwood? It's Dr. Levy."

"And Jim Clarke. Helen's husband. Helen's very worried about you."

"Are you hurt? Sick? Do you need help?"

"Helen wants you to come to our house; she's waiting there for you."

"Listen," the doctor said, and I thought he had his face up very close to the glass, almost touching it. He talked in a very friendly voice, and quietly. "Listen, no one's going to hurt you. We're your friends. We came all the way over here to help you and make sure you were all right and we don't want to bother you. As a matter of fact, we promise not to bother you at all, ever again, if you'll just once say that you're well and safe. Just one word."

"You can't just let people go on worrying and worrying about you," Jim Clarke said.

"Just one word," the doctor said. "All you have to do is say you're all right."

They waited; I could feel them pressing their faces close to the glass, longing to see inside. Constance looked at me across the table and smiled a little, and I smiled back; our safeguards were good and they could not see in.

"Listen," the doctor said, and he raised his voice a little; "listen, Julian's funeral is tomorrow. We thought you'd want to know."

"There are a lot of flowers already," Jim Clarke said. "You'd be really pleased to see all the flowers. We sent flowers, and the Wrights, and the Carringtons. I think you'd feel a little different about your friends if you could see the flowers we all sent Julian."

I wondered why we would feel different if we saw who sent Uncle Julian flowers. Certainly Uncle Julian buried in flowers, swarmed over by flowers, would not resemble the Uncle Julian we had seen every day. Perhaps masses of flowers would warm Uncle Julian dead; I tried to think of Uncle Julian dead and could only remember him asleep. I thought of the Clarkes and the Carringtons and the Wrights pouring armfuls of flowers down onto poor old Uncle Julian, helplessly dead.

"You're not gaining anything by driving away your friends, you know. Helen said to tell you—"

"Listen." I could feel them pushing against the door. "No one's going to bother you. Just tell us, are you all right?"

"We're not going to keep coming, you know. There's a limit to how much friends can take."

Jonas yawned. In silence Constance turned, slowly and carefully, back to face her place at the table, and took up a buttered biscuit and took a tiny silent bite. I wanted to laugh, and put my hands over my mouth; Constance eating a biscuit silently was funny, like a doll pretending to eat.

"*Damn* it," Jim Clarke said. He knocked on the door. "*Damn* it," he said.

"For the last time," the doctor said, "we know you're in there; for the last time will you just—"

"Oh, come away," Jim Clarke said. "It's not worth all the yelling."

"Listen," the doctor said, and I thought he had his mouth against the door, "one of these days you're going to *need* help. You'll be sick, or hurt. You'll *need* help. *Then* you'll be quick enough to—"

"Leave them be," Jim Clarke said. "Come on."

I heard their footsteps going around the side of the house and wondered if they were tricking us, pretending to walk away and then coming silently back to stand without sound outside the door, waiting. I thought of Constance silently eating a biscuit inside and Jim Clarke silently listening outside and a little cold chill went up my back; perhaps there would never be noise in the world again. Then the car started at the front of the house and we heard it drive away and Constance put her fork down on her plate with a little crash and I breathed again and said, "Where have they got Uncle Julian, do you suppose?"

"At that same place," Constance said absently, "in the city. Merricat," she said, looking up suddenly.

"Yes, Constance?"

"I want to say I'm sorry. I was wicked last night."

I was still and cold, looking at her and remembering.

"I was very wicked," she said. "I never should have reminded you of why they all died."

"Then don't remind me now." I could not move my hand to reach over and take hers.

"I wanted you to forget about it. I never wanted to speak about it, ever, and I'm sorry I did."

"I put it in the sugar."

"I know. I knew then."

"You never used sugar."

"No."

"So I put it in the sugar."

Constance sighed. "Merricat," she said, "we'll never talk about it again. Never."

I was chilled, but she smiled at me kindly and it was all right.

"I love you, Constance," I said.

"And I love you, my Merricat."

Jonas sat on the floor and slept on the floor and I thought it ought not to be so difficult for me. Constance should have had leaves and soft moss under her blanket but we could not dirty the kitchen floor again. I put my blanket in the corner near my stool because it was the place I knew best, and Jonas got up onto the stool and sat there, looking down on me. Constance lay on the floor near the stove; it was dark, but I could see the paleness of her face across the kitchen. "Are you comfortable?" I asked her, and she laughed.

"I've spent a lot of time in this kitchen," she said, "but I never before tried lying on its floor. I've taken such good care of it that it has to make me welcome, I think."

"Tomorrow we bring in lettuce."

10

Slowly the pattern of our days grew, and shaped itself into a happy life. In the mornings when I awakened I would go at once down the hall to make sure the front door was locked. We were most active in the very early morning because no one was ever around. We had not realized that, with the gates opened and the path exposed to public use, the children would come; one morning I stood beside the front door, looking out through the narrow pane of glass, and saw children playing on our front lawn. Perhaps the parents had sent them to explore the way and make sure it was navigable, or perhaps children can never resist playing anywhere; they seemed a little uneasy playing in front of our house, and their voices were subdued. I thought that perhaps they were only pretending to play, because they were children and were supposed to play, but perhaps they were actually sent here to look for us, thinly disguised as children. They were not really convincing, I decided as I watched them; they moved gracelessly, and never once glanced, that I could see, at our house. I wondered how soon they would creep onto the porch, and press their small faces against the shutters, trying to see through cracks. Constance came up behind me and looked out over my shoulder. "They are the children of the strangers," I told her. "They have no faces."

"They have eyes."

"Pretend they are birds. They can't see us. They don't know it yet, they don't want to believe it, but they won't ever see us again."

"I suppose that now they've come once, they'll come again."

"All the strangers will come, but they can't see inside. And now may I please have my breakfast?"

The kitchen was always dark in the mornings until I unbolted the kitchen door and opened it to let the sunlight in. Then Jonas went to sit on the step and bathe and Constance sang while she made our breakfast. After breakfast I sat on the step with Jonas while Constance washed the kitchen.

Barricading the sides of the house had been easier than I expected; I managed it in one night with Constance holding a flashlight for me. At either side of our house there was a spot where the trees and bushes grew close to the house, sheltering the back and narrowing the path which was the only way around. I brought piece after piece from the pile of junk Mr. Harler had made on our front porch, and heaped the broken boards and furniture across the narrowest spot. It would not really keep anyone out, of course; the children could climb over it easily, but if anyone did try to get past there would be enough noise and falling of broken boards to give us plenty of time to close and bolt the kitchen door. I had found some boards around the tool shed, and nailed them rudely across the glass of the kitchen door, but I disliked putting them across the sides of the house as a barricade, where anyone might see them and know how clumsily I built. Perhaps, I told myself, I might try my hand at mending the broken step.

"What are you laughing about now?" Constance asked me.

"I am thinking that we are on the moon, but it is not quite as I supposed it would be."

"It is a very happy place, though." Constance was bringing breakfast to the table: scrambled eggs and toasted biscuits and blackberry jam she had made some golden summer. "We ought to bring in as much food as we can," she said. "I don't like to think of the garden waiting there for us to come and gather growing things. And I'd feel much better if we had more food put securely away in the house."

"I will go on my winged horse and bring you cinnamon and thyme, emeralds and clove, cloth of gold and cabbages."

"And rhubarb."

We were able to leave the kitchen door open when we went down to the vegetable garden, because we could see clearly whether anyone was approaching my barricades and run back to the house if we needed to. I carried the basket and we brought back lettuce, still grey with ash, and radishes, and tomatoes and cucumbers and, later, berries, and melons. Usually I ate fruit and vegetables still moist from the ground and the air, but I disliked eating anything while it was still dirty with the ash from our burned house. Most of the dirt and the soot had blown away and the air around the garden was fresh and clean, but the smoke was in the ground and I thought it would always be there.

As soon as we were safely settled Constance had opened Uncle Julian's room and cleaned it. She brought out the sheets from Uncle Julian's bed, and the blankets, and washed them in the kitchen sink and set them outside to dry in the sunlight. "What are you going to do with Uncle Julian's papers?" I asked her, and she rested her hands against the edge of the sink, hesitating.

"I suppose I'll keep them all in the box," she said at last. "I suppose I'll put the box down in the cellar."

"And preserve it?"

"And preserve it. He would like to think that his papers were treated respectfully. And I would not want Uncle Julian to suspect that his papers were not preserved."

"I had better go and see that the front door is locked."

The children were often outside on our front lawn, playing their still games and not looking at our house, moving awkwardly in little dashing runs, and slapping one another without cause. Whenever I checked to make sure that the front door was locked I looked out to see if the children were there. Very often I saw people walking on our path now, using it to go from one place to another, and putting their feet down where once only my feet had gone; I thought they used the path without wanting to, as though each of them had to travel it once to show that it could be done, but I thought that only a few, the defiant hating ones, came by more than once.

I dreamed away the long afternoon while Constance cleaned Uncle Julian's room; I sat on the doorsill with Jonas asleep beside me, and looked out on the quiet safe garden.

"Look, Merricat," Constance said, coming to me with an armful of clothes, "look, Uncle Julian had two suits, and a topcoat and a hat."

"He walked upright once; he told us so himself."

"I can just barely remember him, years ago, going off one day to buy a suit, and I suppose it was one of these suits he bought; they are neither of them much worn."

"What would he have been wearing on the last day with them? What tie did he have on at dinner? He would surely like to have it remembered."

She looked at me for a minute, not smiling. "It would hardly have been one of these; when I came to get him afterwards, at the hospital, he was wearing pajamas and a robe."

"Perhaps he should have one of these suits now."

"He was probably buried in an old suit of Jim Clarke's." Constance started for the cellar, and then stopped. "Merricat?"

"Yes, Constance?"

"Do you realize that these things of Uncle Julian's are the only clothes left in our house? All of mine burned, and all of yours."

"And everything of theirs in the attic."

"I have only this pink dress I have on."

I looked down. "And I am wearing brown."

"And yours needs washing, and mending; how *can* you tear your clothes so, my Merricat?"

"I shall weave a suit of leaves. At once. With acorns for buttons."

"Merricat, be serious. We will have to wear Uncle Julian's clothes."

"I am not allowed to touch Uncle Julian's things. I shall have a lining of moss, for cold winter days, and a hat made of bird feathers."

"That may be all very well for the moon, Miss Foolishness. On the moon you may wear a suit of fur like Jonas, for all of me. But right here in our house you are going to be clothed in one of your Uncle Julian's old shirts, and perhaps his trousers too."

"Or Uncle Julian's bathrobe and pajamas, I suppose. No; I am not allowed to touch Uncle Julian's things; I will wear leaves."

"But you are allowed. I tell you that you are allowed."

"No."

She sighed. "Well," she said, "you'll probably see me wearing them." Then she stopped, and laughed, and looked at me, and laughed again.

"Constance?" I said.

She put Uncle Julian's clothes over the back of a chair, and, still laughing, went into the pantry and opened one of the drawers. I remembered what she was after and I laughed too. Then she came back and put an armload of tablecloths down beside me.

"These will do you very nicely, elegant Merricat. Look; how will you feel in this, with a border of yellow flowers? Or this handsome red and white check? The damask, I am afraid, is too stiff for comfort, and besides it has been darned."

I stood up and held the red and white checked tablecloth against me. "You can cut a hole for my head," I said; I was pleased.

"I have no sewing things. You will simply have to tie it around your waist with a cord or let it hang like a toga."

"I will use the damask for a cloak; who else wears a damask cloak?"

"Merricat, oh, Merricat." Constance dropped the tablecloth she was holding and put her arms around me. "What have I done to my baby Merricat?" she said. "No house. No food. And dressed in a tablecloth; what have I *done*?"

"Constance," I said, "I love you, Constance."

"Dressed in a tablecloth like a rag doll."

"Constance. We are going to be very happy, Constance."

"Oh, Merricat," she said, holding me.

"Listen to me, Constance. We are going to be very happy."

I dressed at once, not wanting to give Constance more time to think. I chose the red and white check, and when Constance had cut a hole for my head I took my gold cord with the tassel that Constance had cut from the drawing-room drapes and tied it around me for a belt and looked, I thought, very fine. Constance was sad at first, and turned away sadly when she saw me, and scrubbed furiously at the sink to get my brown dress clean, but I liked my robe, and danced in it, and before long she smiled again and then laughed at me.

"Robinson Crusoe dressed in the skins of animals," I told her. "He had no gay cloths with a gold belt."

"I must say you never looked so bright before."

"You will be wearing the skins of Uncle Julian; I prefer my tablecloth."

"I believe the one you are wearing now was used for summer breakfasts on the lawn many years ago. Red and white check would never be used in the dining room, of course."

"Some days I shall be a summer breakfast on the lawn, and some days I shall be a formal dinner by candlelight, and some days I shall be—"

"A very dirty Merricat. You have a fine gown, but your face is dirty. We have lost almost everything, young lady, but at least we still have clean water and a comb."

One thing was most lucky about Uncle Julian's room: I persuaded Constance to bring out his chair and wheel it through the garden to reinforce my barricade. It looked strange to see Constance wheeling the empty chair, and for a minute I tried to see Uncle Julian again, riding with his hands in his lap, but all that remained of Uncle Julian's presence were the worn spots on the chair, and a handkerchief tucked under the cushion. The chair would be powerful in my barricade, however, staring out always at intruders with a blank menace of dead Uncle Julian. I was troubled to think that Uncle Julian might vanish altogether, with his papers in a box and his chair on the barricade and his toothbrush thrown away and even the smell of Uncle Julian gone from his room, but when the ground was soft Constance planted a yellow rosebush at Uncle Julian's spot on the lawn, and one night I went down to the creek and buried Uncle Julian's initialled gold pencil by the water, so the creek would always speak his name. Jonas took to going into Uncle Julian's room, where he had never gone before, but I did not go inside.

Helen Clarke came to our door twice more, knocking and calling and begging us to answer, but we sat quietly, and when she found that she could not come around the house because of my barricade she told us from the front door that she would not come back, and she did not. One evening, perhaps the evening of the day Constance planted Uncle Julian's rosebush, we heard a very soft knock at our front door while we sat at the table eating dinner. It was far too soft a knock for Helen Clarke, and I left the table and hurried silently down the hall to be sure that the front door was locked, and Constance followed me, curious. We pressed silently against the door and listened.

"Miss Blackwood?" someone said outside, in a low voice; I wondered if he suspected we were so close to him. "Miss Constance? Miss Mary Katherine?"

It was not quite dark outside, but inside where we stood we could only see one another dimly, two white faces against the door. "Miss Constance?" he said again. "Listen."

I thought that he was moving his head from side to side to make sure that he was not seen. "Listen," he said, "I got a chicken here."

He tapped softly on the door. "I hope you can hear me," he said. "I got a chicken here. My wife fixed it, roasted it nice, and there's some cookies and a pie. I hope you can hear me."

I could see that Constance's eyes were wide with wonder. I stared at her and she stared at me.

"I sure hope you can hear me, Miss Blackwood. I broke one of your chairs and I'm sorry." He tapped against the door again, very softly. "Well," he said. "I'll just set this basket down on your step here. I hope you heard me. Goodbye."

We listened to quiet footsteps going away, and after a minute Constance said, "What shall we do? Shall we open the door?"

"Later," I said. "I'll come when it's really dark."

"I wonder what kind of pie it is. Do you think it's as good as my pies?"

We finished our dinner and waited until I was sure that no one could possibly see the front door opening, and then we went down the hall and I unlocked the door and looked outside. The basket sat on the doorstep, covered with a napkin. I brought it inside and locked the door while Constance took the basket from me and carried it to the kitchen. "Blueberry," she said when I came. "Quite good, too; it's still warm."

She took out the chicken, wrapped in a napkin, and the little package of cookies, touching each lovingly and with gentleness. "Everything's still warm," she said. "She must have baked them right after dinner, so he could bring them right over. I wonder if she made two pies, one for the house. She wrapped everything while it was still warm and told him to bring them over. These cookies are not crisp enough."

"I'll take the basket back and leave it on the porch, so he'll know we found it."

"No, no." Constance caught me by the arm. "Not until I've washed the napkins; what would she think of me?"

Sometimes they brought bacon, home-cured, or fruit, or their own preserves, which were never as good as the preserves Constance made. Mostly they brought roasted chicken; sometimes a cake or a pie, frequently cookies, sometimes a potato salad or coleslaw. Once they brought a pot of beef stew, which Constance took apart and put back together again according to her own rules for beef stew, and sometimes there were pots of baked beans or macaroni. "We are the biggest church supper they ever had," Constance said once, looking at a loaf of home-made bread I had just brought inside.

These things were always left on the front doorstep, always silently and in the evenings. We thought that the men came home from work and the women had the baskets ready for them to carry over; perhaps they came in darkness not to be recognized, as though each of them wanted to hide from the others, and bringing us food was somehow a shameful thing to do in public. There were many women cooking, Constance said. "Here is one," she explained to me once, tasting a bean, "who uses ketchup, and too much of it; and the last one used more molasses." Once or twice there was a note in the basket: "This is for the dishes," or "We apologize about the curtains," or "Sorry for your harp." We always set the baskets back where we had found them, and never opened the front door until it was completely dark and we were sure that no one was near. I always checked carefully afterwards to make certain that the front door was locked.

I discovered that I was no longer allowed to go to the creek; Uncle Julian was there, and it was much too far from Constance. I never went farther away than the edge of the woods, and Constance went only as far as the vegetable garden. I was not allowed to bury anything more, nor was I allowed to touch stone. Every day I looked over the boards across the kitchen windows and when I found small cracks I nailed on more boards. Every morning I checked at once to make sure the front door was locked, and every morning Constance washed the kitchen. We spent a good deal of time at the front door, particularly during the afternoons, when most people came by; we sat, one on either side of the front door, looking out through the narrow glass panels which I had covered almost entirely with cardboard so that we had each only a small peephole and no one could possibly see inside. We watched the children playing, and the people walking past, and we heard their voices and they were all strangers, with their wide staring eyes and their evil open mouths. One day a group came by bicycle; there were two women and a man, and two children. They parked their bicycles in our driveway and lay down on our front lawn, pulling at the grass and talking while they rested. The children ran up and down our driveway and over and around the trees and bushes. This was the day that we learned that the vines were growing over the burned roof of our house, because one of the women glanced sideways at the house and said that the vines almost hid the marks of burning. They rarely turned squarely to look at our house face to face, but looked from the corners of their eyes or from over a shoulder or through their fingers. "It used to be a lovely old house, I hear," said the woman sitting on our grass. "I've heard that it was quite a local landmark at one time."

"Now it looks like a tomb," the other woman said.

"Shh," the first woman said, and gestured toward the house with her head. "I heard," she said loudly, "that they had a staircase which was very fine. Carved in Italy, I heard."

"They can't hear you," the other woman said, amused. "And who cares if they do, anyway?"

"Shhh."

"No one knows for sure if there's anyone inside or not. The local people tell some tall tales."

"Shh. Tommy," she called to one of the children, "don't you go near those steps."

"Why?" said the child, backing away.

"Because the ladies live in there, and they don't like it."

"Why?" said the child, pausing at the foot of the steps and giving a quick look backward at our front door.

"The ladies don't like little boys," the second woman said; she was one of the bad ones; I could see her mouth from the side and it was the mouth of a snake.

"What would they do to me?"

"They'd hold you down and make you eat candy full of poison; I heard that dozens of bad little boys have gone too near that house and never been seen again. They catch little boys and they—"

"Shh. *Honestly,* Ethel."

"Do they like little girls?" The other child drew near.

"They hate little boys *and* little girls. The difference is, they *eat* the little girls."

"Ethel, stop. You're terrifying the children. It isn't true, darlings; she's only teasing you."

"They never come out except at night," the bad woman said, looking evilly at the children, "and then when it's dark they go hunting little children."

"Just the same," the man said suddenly, "I don't want to see the kids going too near that house."

Charles Blackwood came back only once. He came in a car with another man late one afternoon when we had been watching for a long time. All the strangers had gone, and Constance had just stirred and said, "Time to put on the potatoes," when the car turned into the driveway and she settled back to watch again. Charles and the other man got out of the car in front of the house and walked directly to the foot of the steps, looking up, although they could not see us inside. I remembered the first time Charles had come and stood looking up at our house in just the same manner, but this time he would never get in. I reached up and touched the lock on the front door to make sure it was fastened, and on the other side of the doorway Constance turned and nodded to me; she knew, too, that Charles would never get in again.

"See?" Charles said, outside, at the foot of our steps. "There's the house, just like I said. It doesn't look as bad as it did, now the vines have grown so. But the roof's been burned away, and the place was gutted inside."

"Are the ladies in there?"

"Sure." Charles laughed, and I remembered his laughter and his big staring white face and from inside the door I wished him dead. "They're in there all right," he said. "And so is a whole damn fortune."

"You *know* that?"

"They've got money in there's never even been counted. They've got it buried all over, and a safe full, and God knows where else they've hidden it. They never come out, just hide away inside with all that money."

"Look," the other man said, "they know you, don't they?"

"Sure. I'm their cousin. I came here on a visit once."

"You think there's any chance you might get one of them to talk to you? Maybe come to the window or something, so I could get a picture?"

Charles thought. He looked at the house and at the other man, and thought. "If you sell this, to the magazine or somewhere, do I get half?"

"Sure, it's a promise."

"I'll try it," Charles said. "You get back behind the car, out of sight. They certainly won't come out if they see a stranger." The other man went back to the car and took out a camera and settled himself on the other side of the car where we could not see him. "Okay," he called, and Charles started up the steps to our front door.

"Connie?" he called. "Hey, Connie? It's Charles; I'm back."

I looked at Constance and thought she had never seen Charles so truly before.

"Connie?"

She knew now that Charles was a ghost and a demon, one of the strangers.

"Let's forget all that happened," Charles said. He came close to the door and spoke pleasantly, with a little pleading tone. "Let's be friends again."

I could see his feet. One of them was tapping and tapping on the floor of our porch. "I don't know what you've got against me," he said, "and I've been waiting and waiting for you to let me know I could come back again. If I did anything to offend you, I'm really sorry."

I wished Charles could see inside, could see us sitting on the floor on either side of the front door, listening to him and looking at his feet, while he talked beggingly to the door three feet above our heads.

"Open the door," he said very softly. "Connie, will you open the door for me, for Cousin Charles?"

Constance looked up to where his face must be and smiled unpleasantly. I thought it must be a smile she had been saving for Charles if he ever came back again.

"I went to see old Julian's grave this morning," Charles said. "I came back to visit old Julian's grave and to see you once more." He waited a minute and then said with a little break in his voice, "I put a couple of flowers—*you* know—on the old fellow's grave; he was a fine old guy, and he was always pretty good to me."

Beyond Charles' feet I saw the other man coming out from behind the car with his camera. "Look," he called, "you're wasting your breath. And I haven't got all day."

"Don't you understand?" Charles had turned away from the door, but his voice still had the little break in it. "I've *got* to see her once more. I was the cause of it all."

"What?"

"Why do you suppose two old maids shut themselves up in a house like this? God knows," Charles said, "I didn't mean it to turn out this way."

I thought Constance was going to speak then, or at least laugh out loud, and I reached across and touched her arm, warning her to be quiet, but she did not turn her head to me.

"If I could just *talk* to her," Charles said. "You can get some pictures of the house, anyway, with me standing here. Or knocking at the door; I could be knocking frantically at the door."

"You could be stretched across the doorsill dying of a broken heart, for all of me," the other man said. He went to the car and put his camera inside. "Waste of time."

"And all that money. Connie," Charles called loudly, "will you for heaven's sake open that door?"

"You know," the other man said from the car, "I'll just bet you're never going to see those silver dollars again."

"Connie," Charles said, "you don't know what you're doing to me; I never deserved to be treated like this. *Please*, Connie."

"You want to walk back to town?" the other man said. He closed the car door.

Charles turned away from the door and then turned back. "All right, Connie," he said, "this is it. If you let me go this time, you'll never see me again. I mean it, Connie."

"I'm leaving," the other man said from the car.

"I mean it, Connie, I really do." Charles started down the steps, talking over his shoulder. "Take a last look," he said. "I'm going. One word could make me stay."

I did not think he was going to go in time. I honestly did not know whether Constance was going to be able to contain herself until he got down the steps and safely into the car. "Goodbye, Connie," he said from the foot of the steps and then turned away and went slowly toward the car. He looked for a minute as though he might wipe his eyes or blow his nose, but the other man said, "Hurry *up*," and Charles looked back once more, raised his hand sadly, and got into the car. Then Constance laughed, and I laughed, and for a minute I saw Charles in the car turn his head quickly, as though he had heard us laughing, but the car started, and drove off down the driveway, and we held each other in the dark hall and laughed, with the tears running down our cheeks and echoes of our laughter going up the ruined stairway to the sky.

"I am so happy," Constance said at last, gasping. "Merricat, I am so happy."

"I told you that you would like it on the moon."

The Carringtons stopped their car in front of our house one Sunday after church and sat quietly in the car looking at our house, as though supposing that we would come out if there was anything the Carringtons could do for us. Sometimes I thought of the drawing room and the dining room, forever closed away, with our mother's lovely broken things lying scattered, and the dust sifting gently down to cover them; we had new landmarks in the house, just as we had a new pattern for our days. The crooked, broken-off fragment which was all that was left of our lovely stairway was something we passed every day and came to know as intimately as we had once known the stairs themselves. The boards across the kitchen windows were ours, and part of our house, and we loved them. We were very happy, although Constance was always in terror lest one of our two cups should break, and one of us have to use a cup without a handle. We had our well-known and familiar places: our chairs at the table, and our beds, and our places beside the front door. Constance washed the red and white tablecloth and the shirts of Uncle Julian's which she wore, and while they were hanging in the garden to dry I wore a tablecloth with a yellow border, which looked very handsome with my gold belt. Our mother's old brown shoes were safely put away in my corner of the kitchen, since in the warm summer days I went barefoot like Jonas. Constance disliked picking many flowers, but there was always a bowl on the kitchen table with roses or daisies, although of course she never picked a rose from Uncle Julian's rosebush.

I sometimes thought of my six blue marbles, but I was not allowed to go to the long field now, and I thought that perhaps my six blue marbles had been buried to protect a house which no longer existed and had no connection with the house where we lived now, and where we were very happy. My new magical safeguards were the lock on the front door, and the boards over the windows, and the barricades along the sides of the

house. In the evenings sometimes we saw movement in the darkness on the lawn, and heard whispers.

"Don't; the ladies might be watching."

"You think they can see in the dark?"

"I heard they see everything that goes on."

Then there might be laughter, drifting away into the warm
darkness.

"They will soon be calling this Lover's Lane," Constance said.

"After Charles, no doubt."

"The least Charles could have done," Constance said, con-
sidering seriously, "was shoot himself through the head in the
driveway."

We learned, from listening, that all the strangers could see
from outside, when they looked at all, was a great ruined struc-
ture overgrown with vines, barely recognizable as a house. It
was the point halfway between the village and the highway, the
middle spot on the path, and no one ever saw our eyes looking
out through the vines.

"You can't go on those steps," the children warned each
other; "if you do, the ladies will get you."

Once a boy, dared by the others, stood at the foot of the steps
facing the house, and shivered and almost cried and almost ran
away, and then called out shakily, "Merricat, said Constance,
would you like a cup of tea?" and then fled, followed by all the
others. That night we found on the doorsill a basket of fresh
eggs and a note reading, "He didn't mean it, please."

"Poor child," Constance said, putting the eggs into a bowl
to go into the cooler. "He's probably hiding under the bed
right now."

"Perhaps he had a good whipping to teach him manners."

"We will have an omelette for breakfast."

"I wonder if I *could* eat a child if I had the chance."

"I doubt if I could cook one," said Constance.

"Poor strangers," I said. "They have so much to be afraid of."

"Well," Constance said, "I am afraid of spiders."

"Jonas and I will see to it that no spider ever comes near you.
Oh, Constance," I said, "we are so happy."

Shirley Jackson's Witchcraft: *We Have Always Lived in the Castle*

"We eat the year away. We eat the
spring and the summer and the fall.
We wait for something to grow and then we eat it."
(Merricat, *We Have Always Lived in the Castle*, p. 45)

Of the precocious children and adolescents of mid-twentieth-century American fiction—a dazzling lot that includes the tomboys Frankie of Carson McCullers's *The Member of the Wedding* (1946) and Scout of Harper Lee's *To Kill a Mocking Bird* (1960), the murderous eight-year-old Rhoda Penmark of William March's *The Bad Seed* (1954), and the slightly older, disaffected Holden Caulfield of J. D. Salinger's *The Catcher in the Rye* (1951) and Esther Greenwood of Sylvia Plath's *The Bell Jar* (1963)—none is more memorable than eighteen-year-old "Merricat" of Shirley Jackson's masterpiece of gothic suspense, *We Have Always Lived in the Castle* (1962). At once feral child, sulky adolescent, and Cassandra-like seer, Merricat addresses the reader as an intimate:

> My name is Mary Katherine Blackwood. I am eighteen years old, and I live with my sister Constance. I have often thought that with any luck at all I could have been born a werewolf, because the two middle fingers on both my hands are the same length, but I have had to be content with what I had. I dislike washing myself, and dogs, and noise. I like my sister Constance, and Richard Plantagenet, and *Amanita phalloides,* the death-cup mushroom. Everyone else in my family is dead. (p. 1)

Merricat speaks with a seductive and disturbing authority, never drawn to justifying her actions but only to recounting them. One might expect *We Have Always Lived in the Castle* to be a confession, of a kind—after all, one or another of the Blackwood sisters poisoned their entire family, six years before—but Merricat has nothing to confess, still less to regret; *We Have Always Lived in the Castle* is a romance with an improbable—magical—happy ending. As readers we are led to smile at Merricat's childish self-definition, as one who dislikes "washing myself"; it will be many pages before we come to realize the significance of *Amanita phalloides* and the wish to have been born a werewolf. In this deftly orchestrated opening, Merricat's wholly sympathetic creator/collaborator Shirley Jackson has struck every essential note of her gothic tale of sexual repression and rhapsodic vengeance; as it unfolds in ways both inevitable and unexpected, *We Have Always Lived in the Castle* becomes a New England fairy tale of the more wicked variety, in which a "happy ending" is both ironic and literal, the consequence of unrepentant witchcraft and a terrible sacrifice—of others.

Like other, similarly isolated and estranged hypersensitive young female protagonists of Shirley Jackson's fiction—Natalie of *Hangsaman* (1951), Elizabeth of *The Bird's Nest* (1954), Eleanor of *The Haunting of Hill House* (1959)—Merricat is socially maladroit, highly self-conscious and disdainful of others. She is "special"—her witchery appears to be self-invented, an expression of desperation and a yearning to stop time with no connection to satanic practices, still less to Satan. (Merricat is too willful a witch to align herself with a putative higher power, especially a masculine power.) Her voice is sharp, funny, compelling—and teasing. For more than one hundred pages Merricat taunts us with what she knows, and we don't know; her recounting of the tragic Blackwood family history is piecemeal, as in the tangled back-story there is an echo of Henry James's *The Turn of the Screw*—that masterwork of unreliable narration in which we are intimate witnesses to a naively repressed young woman's voyeuristic experience of sexual transgression and "exquisite pathos." Like the innocent, pubescent girl protagonists of *The Member of the Wedding* and *To Kill a Mockingbird*, Merricat Blackwood appears to be a typical product of small town rural America—much of her time is

spent outdoors, alone with her companion cat Jonas; she's a
tomboy who wanders in the woods, unwashed and her hair
uncombed; she's distrustful of adults, and of authority; despite
being uneducated, she is shrewdly intelligent, and bookish. At
times Merricat behaves as if mildly retarded, but only out-
wardly; inwardly, she's razorsharp in her observations, and
hyperalert to threats to her wellbeing. (Like any damaged person Merricat most fears change in the unvarying rituals of her
household.) A mysterious amalgam of the childlike and the
treacherous, Merricat is "domesticated" by only one person,
her older sister Constance.

"Wear your boots if you wander today," Constance told
me.
[. . .]
"I love you, Constance," I said.
"I love you too, silly Merricat." (p. 51)

There is a lovely lyricism to her observations when she's
alone, and out of doors:

The day outside was full of changing light, and Jonas
danced in and out of shadows as he followed me . . . We
were going to the long field which today looked like an
ocean, although I had never seen an ocean; the grass
was moving in the breeze and the cloud shadows passed
back and forth and the trees in the distance moved
[. . . .] I am walking on buried treasure, I thought, with
the grass brushing against my hands and nothing around
me but the reach of the long field with the grass blowing
and the pine woods at the end; behind me was the house,
and far off to my left, hidden by trees and almost out of
sight, was the wire fence our father had built to keep
people out. (p. 52—3)

Even in this pastoral setting Merricat is brought back forcibly
to the prejudices of her upbringing: the Blackwoods' contempt
for others.

If Merricat is mad, it's a "poetic" madness like the madness of the young heroine of *The Bird's Nest*, whose subdued personality harbours several selves, or the madness celebrated by Emily Dickinson—"Much Madness is divinest Sense—/ To a discerning Eye—/ Much sense—the starkest Madness—'Tis the Majority" Merricat's condition suggests paranoid schizophrenia, in which anything out of the ordinary is likely to be threatening and all things are signs and symbols to be deciphered—"All the omens spoke of change" (p. 40). Merricat is determined to deflect "change"—the threat to her household—through witchcraft, a kind of simple, sympathetic magic involving "safeguards": ". . .the box of silver dollars I had buried by the creek, and the doll buried in the long field, and the book nailed to the tree in the pine woods; as long as they were where I had put them nothing could get in to harm us" (p. 41). Merricat—surely like her creator—is one for whom words are highly potent, as well:

> On Sunday morning the change was one day nearer. I was resolute about not thinking my three magic words and would not let them into my mind, but the air of change was so strong that there was no avoiding it; change lay over the stairs and the kitchen and the garden like fog. I would not forget my magic words; they were MELODY GLOUCESTER PEGASUS, but I refused to let them into my mind. (p. 51)

By degrees we learn that there are many household tasks that Merricat isn't allowed to do, like help in the preparation of food or handle knives. Minor frustrations have a violent effect upon her: "I could not breathe; I was tied with wire, and my head was huge and going to explode . . . I had to content myself with smashing the milk pitcher which waited on the table; it had been our mothers, and I left the pieces on the floor so that Constance would see them" (p. 27). It's ironic that Merricat's aristocratic disdain of other people derives from her identification with her rich New England family—now nearly extinct—whom she seems to have hated violently

when they were alive. It may have been her parents' disciplin-
ing of her that precipitated the family tragedy when, as Uncle
Julian reminisces, Merricat was "A great child of twelve, sent
to bed without her supper" (p. 34).

In the novel's opening, suspenseful chapter, Merricat must
make her way from the Blackwood manor house at the edge of
the village into town, as the intermediary between the remaining Blackwoods and the outer world: "Fridays and Tuesdays
were terrible days, because I had to go into the village. Someone had to go to the library, and the grocery; Constance never
went past her own garden, and Uncle Julian could not" (p. 2).
Here is no Grover's Corners as in Thornton Wilder's senti-
mental classic of small town America, *Our Town*: this is a
New England town of "dirty little houses on the main highway" (p. 4)—a place of unmitigated "ugliness" and "rot" (p. 6)
where dwell individuals poised to "come at [Merricat] like a
flock of taloned hawks—birds descending, striking, gashing
with razor claws" (p. 7). Hostility toward the Blackwoods
seems to have predated the Blackwood poisoning scandal:

The people of the village have always hated us. (p.4)

The blight on the village never came from the Blackwoods;
the villagers belonged here and the village was the only
proper place for them.

I always thought about rot when I came toward the
row of stores; I thought about burning black painful rot
that ate away from inside, hurting dreadfully. I wished it
on the village. (p. 6)

Merricat's fantasies are childish, alarmingly sadistic: "I am
walking on their bodies" (p. 10)—"I am going to put death in
all their food and watch them die." (p. 10) —"I would have
liked to come into the grocery some morning and see them all,
even the Elberts and the children, lying there crying with the
pain and dying. I would then help myself to groceries . . . stepping over their bodies, taking whatever I fancied from the
shelves" (p. 9). Such unmitigated hatred, out of all proportion

to any source within *We Have Always Lived in the Castle,* suggests a savage Swiftian indignation that passes beyond social
satire of the kind written by Jackson's older contemporaries,
Sinclair Lewis and H. L. Mencken, into the realm of psycho-
pathological caricature. (Jackson's difficulties with her fellow
citizens in North Bennington, Vermont are well documented in
Judy Oppenheimer's harrowing biography, *Private Demons,*
(1988): the suggestion is that Jackson and her husband, the
flamboyant "Jewish-intellectual" cultural critic Stanley Edgar
Hyman aroused resentment, if not outright anti-Semitism, in
their more conventional Christian neighbours.) The animosity
of the villagers for the Blackwoods suggests the priggish racism
of Jackson's subtly modulated short story "Flower Garden"—
in which a newcomer to a New England village unwisely
befriends a resident black man—and the barbaric behaviour of
the villagers of Jackson's most famous story, "The Lottery", in
which a yearly ritual of scapegoating and stoning to death is
enacted by lottery. Here, in a place said to closely resemble the
North Bennington of Shirley Jackson's day, a dirge-like tune of
unknown origin prevails from generation to generation, unques-
tioned by the brainless local citizenry:

> Lottery in June, corn be heavy soon.

In *We Have Always Lived in the Castle,* a jeering chant follows
in Merricat's wake when she ventures into town:

> Merricat, said Connie, would you like a cup of tea?
> Oh, no, said Merricat, you'll poison me. (p. 17)

In the village, life is crude, cruel, noisy and ugly; in the Blackwood manor house, life is quiet, sequestered, governed by the
daily custom and ritual of mealtimes, above all inward—"almost
all of our life was lived toward the back of the house, on the
lawn and the garden where no one else ever came . . . The rooms
we used together were the back ones" (p. 20). The Blackwood
house isn't haunted in quite the way that Hill House is haunted—
("No live organism can continue for long to exist sanely under

conditions of absolute reality. Hill House, not sane, stood by itself against its hills, holding darkness within. . ." (*The Haunting of Hill House,* p. 1) but its former, now deceased inhabitants emerge in portentous times, in Merricat's sleep, calling her name—to warn her? To torment her? By degrees we discover the secret of the Blackwood house—the poisonings, by arsenic, six years before, of the entire family except Constance, then twenty-two years old, Merricat, then twelve, and their Uncle Julian. Constance, who'd prepared the meal that day, and took care to wash out the sugar bowl before police arrived, was accused of the poisonings, tried and acquitted, for lack of sufficient evidence; Merricat was sent away for the duration of the trial, then brought back to live with Constance and her uncle in their diminished household. (Julian, who has never recovered from the trauma of arsenic poisoning, persists in believing that Merricat died in the "orphanage"—despite the fact that he and his niece inhabit the same house.) Merricat's uncle is preoccupied with writing up his account of the poisonings:

> "In some ways, [. . .] a piece of extraordinarily good fortune for me. I am a survivor of the most sensational poisoning case of the century. I have all the newspaper clippings. I knew the victims, the accused, intimately, as only a relative living in the house *could* know them. I have exhaustive notes on all that happened. I have never been well since." (p. 32)

Why no one seems to suspect—as the reader does, immediately— that the unstable Merricat, not the amiable Constance, is the poisoner is one of the curiosities of the novel, as it's a mystery why Constance is so indulgent of Merricat, who contributes nothing to the household. Certainly there's little subterfuge in Merricat's teasing of others, in alluding to various kinds of poisons; her tormenting of her cousin Charles contains a transparent threat:

> "The *Amanita phalloides,*" I said to [Charles], "holds three different poisons. There is amanitin, which works

slowly and is most potent. There is phalloidin, which acts at once, and there is phallin, which dissolves red corpuscles ... The symptoms begin with violent stomach pains, cold sweat, vomiting ... Death occurs between five and ten days after eating." (p. 72—73)

Constance's mild reproach: "Silly Merricat."

In much of Shirley Jackson's fiction food is fetishized to an extraordinary degree; ironic then, that the Blackwood family should be poisoned by one of their own, out of a family heirloom sugar bowl. That the food fetish has its erotic component is suggested by the means of poison—*Amanita phalloides*—and by the way Merricat so totally depends upon her older sister as a food provider, as if she were an unweaned infant and not a "great child" grown into an adult. Sexual attraction *per se* is virtually nonexistent in Jackson's fiction: the single sexual episode in all of her work appears to be a molestation of some kind, short of rape, that occurs in an early scene of *Hangsaman*—"Oh my dear God sweet Christ, Natalie thought, so sickened she nearly said it aloud, is he going to *touch* me?"—but the episode isn't described, and is never acknowledged by the afflicted young woman, who gradually succumbs to schizophrenia. Nowhere in Jackson's work is food more elaborately fetishized than in *We Have Always Lived in the Castle*, in which the three remaining members of a once-aristocratic family have virtually nothing to do but inhabit their blighted house and "eat the year away" (p. 45) in meals which the older sister prepares for them, three times a day, like clockwork; as in a gothic parody of the comical self-portraits Jackson created for the women's magazine market in the 1950s, in such bestselling books as *Life Among the Savages* (1953) and *Raising Demons* (1956)—a housewife-mother's frustrations transformed, as by a deft twist of the wrist, into, not a grim account of disintegration and madness, still less the poisoning of her family, but light-hearted comedy. (It's ironic to note that Shirley Jackson died at the age of forty-nine, shortly after the publication of *We Have Always Lived in the Castle*, of amphetamine addiction, alcoholism and morbid obesity; negligent of her health for years, she is said to have spoken openly of not expecting to live to be fifty, and in the final months of her life suffered from agoraphobia so extreme she couldn't leave her squalid bedroom—as if in mimicry of the agoraphobic sisters of *We Have Always Lived in the Castle.)*

As Merricat has uneasily sensed, "change" is imminent, and will bring with it the invasion of the Blackwood household. Without having been invited, the sisters' boorish cousin Charles arrives, intent upon stealing their deceased father's money, which he believes to be in a safe; he dares to take Mr Blackwood's position at the head of the dining room table—"He even *looks* like father," Constance says. Unwisely, Charles threatens his young cousin Merricat: "I haven't quite decided what I'm going to do with you [. . .] But whatever I do, you'll remember it" (p. 90). It's a measure of Constance's desperation that though Charles is not a very attractive man, she appears drawn to him, as a way into a possible new life, a prospect terrifying to Merricat. Yet the slightest wish on Constance's part for something other than her stultifying robot-life and Merricat reacts threateningly, for the sisters' secret is the intimate bond between them that sets them apart from all of the world. Throughout the novel there is the prevailing threat of the murderous Merricat whose fantasy life is obsessed with rituals of power, dominance, and revenge: "bow your heads to our beloved Mary Katherine . . . . or you will be dead" (p. 111).

The hideous arsenic deaths constitute the secret heart of *We Have Always Lived in the Castle*, as unspecified sexual acts appear to be at the heart of *The Turn of the Screw*: the taboo yet irresistible subject upon which all thinking, all speech, all actions turn. The sisters are linked forever by the deaths of their family, as in a quasi-spiritual-incestuous bond by which each holds the other in thrall. Food shopping (by Merricat), food preparation (by Constance), and food consumption (by both) is the sacred, or erotic ritual that binds them, even after the house has been partly demolished by fire and they are living in its ruins:

"It is a very happy place, though." Constance was bringing breakfast to the table: scrambled eggs and toasted biscuits and blackberry jam she had made some golden
summer. "We ought to bring in as much food as we can,"
she said [. . .]

"I will go on my winged horse and bring you cinnamon
and thyme, emeralds and clove, cloth of gold and cabbages". (p. 133).

Witchcraft is a primitive attempt at science; an attempt to assert
power by the powerless. Traditionally witchcraft, like voodoo,
and spiritualism, has been the province of marginal individuals
of whom most are women and girls. In Jackson's novel of mul-
tiple personalities, *The Bird's Nest,* the afflicted young heroine's
psychiatrist—aptly named Dr Wright—tries to explicate the
bizarre psychic phenomena he has been trying to "cure":

"Each life, I think [. . .] asks the devouring of other lives
for its own continuance; the radical aspect of ritual sacrifice, the performance of a group, its great step ahead, was
in organization; sharing the victim was so eminently practical . . . (*The Magic of Shirley Jackson, p.* 378)

The doctor spoke slowly, in a measured voice [. . .] : "The
human creature at odds with its environment [. . .] must
change either its own protective coloration, or the shape
of the world in which it lives. Equipped with no magic
device beyond [. . .] intelligence [. . .] the human creature
finds its tempting to endeavor to control its surroundings
through manipulated symbols of sorcery, arbitrarily chosen, and frequently ineffectual." *(The Magic of Shirley
Jackson,* p. 379)

Jackson is rarely so explicit in her thematic intentions: it's as if
her literary-critic/ English professor husband Stanley Edgar
Hyman were lecturing to her, in a manner that sounds like mild
self-parody even as it helps to illuminate both the tangled *Bird's
Nest* and the ruined *Castle.*

After Merricat sets a fire in the Blackwood house in the hope of expelling her detested cousin Charles, the yet more detested villagers swarm onto the private property. Some are firemen who seem sincere in their responsibility of putting out the fire but most want to see the Blackwood house destroyed: "Why not let it burn?"—"Let it burn!" (p. 104). The jeering rhyme is heard, a new line added:

> "Merricat, said Constance, would you like a cup of tea?"
> "Merricat, said Constance, would you like to go to sleep?"
> 'Oh, no, said Merricat, you'll poison me." (p. 107)

Radical change has swept upon the Blackwoods, ironically through the agency of Merricat. The fire she sets causes the death of Uncle Julian, the sisters are forced to flee into the woods, villagers enter the private residence and vandalize it. Yet, when the sisters return, in a tenderly elegiac scene, they discover that though most of the rooms are uninhabitable, all they require—a kitchen, primarily, where Constance can continue to prepare meals for Merricat—has been left intact. As if by magic the old house has been transformed: "Our house was a castle, turreted and open to the sky" (p. 120). Against all expectations the Blackwood sisters are happy in their private paradise "on the moon" (p. 133).

> "I love you, Constance," I said.
> "And I love you, my Merricat," Constance said. (p. 130)

Constance has succumbed to Merricat entirely: the "good" sister has yielded to the "evil" sister. Constance even berates herself for being "wicked"—"I should never have reminded you of why they all died" (p. 130)—in this way acknowledging her complicity in the deaths. Now we understand why Constance never accused Merricat of the poisonings or made any attempt to defend herself against accusations that she was the murderer for, in her heart, she *was* and *is* the Blackwoods' murderer, and not Merricat; that is, not only Merricat. Her acknowledgment tacitly guarantees the sisters' permanent expulsion from the world of normal people—a world in which the psychologically damaged Merricat could not survive. *We Have Always Lived in the Castle* ends on an unexpectedly idyllic note like a fairy-tale romance in which lovers have found each other and even the villagers, repentant of their cruelty, pay the Blackwood sisters homage by bringing food offerings to them, left at the ruins of their doorstep: "Sometimes they brought bacon, home-cured, or fruit, or their own preserves ... Mostly they brought roasted chicken; sometimes a cake or a pie, frequently cookies, sometimes a potato salad or coleslaw ... Sometimes pots of baked beans or macaroni" (p. 139). Here is the very Eros of food, an astonishing wish-fulfillment fantasy in which the agoraphobic is not pitied but revered, idolized; the destruction of her house isn't death to her, but a new life protected by magic: "My new magical safeguards were the lock on the front door, and the boards over the windows, and the barricades along the sides of the house" (p. 145). Repeatedly as in a rapture Merricat cries, "Oh, Constance, we are so happy." The sisters' jokes are slyly food-oriented, of course:

"I wonder if I *could* eat a child if I had the chance."
"I doubt if I could cook one," said Constance. (p. 146)

Joyce Carol Oates, 2009

THE BIRD'S NEST

Shirley Jackson

'Ever since Betsy had been a prisoner she had watched while Elizabeth slept ... seeing the dim figures of Elizabeth's world when Elizabeth's eyes were open, and the screaming phantoms of Elizabeth's nightmares'

Elizabeth Richmond is almost too quiet to be believed, with no friends, no parents, and a job that leaves her strangely unnoticed. But soon she starts to behave in ways she can neither control nor understand, to the increasing horror of her doctor, and the humiliation of her self-centred aunt. As a tormented Elizabeth becomes two people, then three, then four, each wilder and more wicked than the last, a battle of wills threatens to destroy the girl and all who surround her. *The Bird's Nest* is a macabre journey into who we are, and how close we sometimes come to the brink of madness.

HANGSAMAN

Shirley Jackson

Natalie Waite, a daughter of a mediocre writer and a neurotic house-wife, is increasingly unsure of her place in the world. In the midst of adolescence, she senses a creeping darkness in her life, which will spread among nightmarish parties, poisonous college cliques and the manipulations of the intellectual men who surround her, as her identity gradually crumbles.

Inspired by the unsolved disappearance of a female college student near Shirley Jackson's home, *Hangasman* is a story of lurking disquiet and haunting disorientation.

'A leader in the field of beautifully written, quiet, cumulative shudders' Dorothy Parker

JUST AN ORDINARY DAY

Shirley Jackson

A college student receives a diabolical visitor. Two little girls watch a child through a bedroom window. Malice and poison lurk beneath an elderly lady's perfect rose bushes ... A shudder runs through many of the stories in this collection from Shirley Jackson. From twisted tales of modern Bluebeards and Jack the Rippers to poetic fables and wry family dramas, *Just an Ordinary Day* shows the remarkable range of her writing, capturing the unease behind everyday American life with glittering brilliance.

'Jackson at her best ... a gift to a new generation' *San Francisco Chronicle*

THE ROAD THROUGH THE WALL

Shirley Jackson

In Pepper Street, an attractive suburban neighbourhood filled with bullies and egotistical bigots, the feelings of the inhabitants are shallow and selfish: what can a neighbour do to triumph over another neighbour, what may be won from a friend? One child stands alone in her goodness: little Caroline Desmond, kind, sweet and gentle, and the pride of her family. But the malice and self-absorption of the people of Pepper Street lead to a terrible event that will destroy the community of which they are so proud.

Exposing the murderous cruelty of children, and the blindness and selfishness of adults, Shirley Jackson reveals the ugly truth behind a 'perfect' world.

'An unburnished exercise in the sinister' *The New York Times*

THE HAUNTING OF HILL HOUSE

Shirley Jackson

Four seekers have arrived at the rambling old pile known as Hill House: Dr. Montague, an occult scholar looking for solid evidence of psychic phenomena; Theodora, his lovely and lighthearted assistant; Luke, the adventurous future inheritor of the estate; and Eleanor, a friendless, fragile young woman with a dark past. As they begin to cope with chilling, even horrifying occurrences beyond their control or understanding, they cannot possibly know what lies ahead. For Hill House is gathering its powers – and soon it will choose one of them to make its own.

'Stepping into Hill House is like stepping into the mind of a madman; it isn't long before you weird yourself out' Stephen King

THE NIGHT MANAGER

John le Carré

At the start of it all, Jonathan Pine is merely the night manager at a luxury hotel. But when a single attempt to pass on information to the British authorities – about an international businessman at the hotel with suspicious dealings – backfires terribly, and people close to Pine begin to die, he commits himself to a battle against powerful forces he cannot begin to imagine.

In a chilling tale of corrupt intelligence agencies, billion-dollar price tags and the truth of the brutal arms trade, John le Carré creates a claustrophobic world in which no one can be trusted.

'A marvellously observed relentless tale' *Observer*

THE OUTSIDER

Albert Camus

'The sky seemed to rip apart from end to end to pour fire down upon me'

Meursault will not conform. When his mother dies, he refuses to show his emotions simply to satisfy the expectations of others. And when he commits a random act of violence on a sun-drenched beach, his lack of remorse only compounds his guilt in the eyes of society and the law.

Albert Camus' portrayal of a man confronting the absurdity of human life became an existentialist classic. Yet it is also a book filled with quiet joy in the 'tender indifference' of the physical world, and this new translation based on listening to a recording of Camus reading aloud, sensitively renders the subtleties and dreamlike atmosphere of *The Outsider*.

'A dense and rich creation, full of undiscovered meanings and formal qualities' Carl Viggiani

THE PLAGUE

Albert Camus

'This empty town, white with dust, saturated with sea smells, loud with the howl of the wind'

The townspeople of Oran are in the grip of a deadly plague, which condemns its victims to a swift and horrifying death. Fear, isolation and claustrophobia follow as they are forced into quarantine. Each person responds in their own way to the lethal disease: some resign themselves to fate, some seek blame, and a few, like Dr Rieux, resist the terror.

An immediate triumph when it was published in 1947, The Plague is in part an allegory of France's suffering under the Nazi occupation, and a story of bravery and determination against the precariousness of human existence.

'Enduring fiction has the power to grow into new kinds of timeliness' Boyd Tonkin, *Independent*

MRS BRIDGE

Evan S. Connell

Mrs Bridge is a housewife and mother in Kansas City, bringing up her three children and making a home for her husband, Walter. She shops, plays bridge and goes to the country club, but as time passes she finds that her life is unfulfilling and she cannot even ask herself the questions that trouble her. And while the children grow up and become strangers to her, Mrs Bridge – kind yet bigoted, rich yet simple – is left uncertain of her place in the world.

In a series of comical, subtle and shattering vignettes, Evan S. Connell captures perfectly the contradictions, narrow margins and fear that can shadow a life of comfort.

'Very, very funny, often moving and sad, and written with an uncompromising realism that one rarely comes across' *Daily Telegraph*

THE BALLAD OF THE SAD CAFÉ

Carson McCullers

Few writers have expressed loneliness, the need for human understanding and the search for love with such power and poetic sensibility as the American writer Carson McCullers.

In *The Ballad of the Sad Café*, a tale of unrequited love, Miss Amelia, a spirited, unconventional woman, runs a smalltown store and, except for a marriage that lasted just ten days, has always lived alone. Then Cousin Lymon appears from nowhere, a little, strutting hunchback who steals Miss Amelia's heart. Together they transform the store into a lively, popular café. But when her rejected husband Marvin Macy returns, the result is a bizarre love triangle that brings with it violence, hatred and betrayal.

Six stories by Carson McCullers also appear in this volume.

'Enchanting . . . an exquisite talent' *Sunday Times*